Opal Fields

Her
Buried
Bones

Chapter 1

The air seared... hot like an oven as Constable Williams disembarked the thirty-four-seater aircraft that transported her from her hometown to this dry, barren landscape in the centre of South Australia.

She tossed her backpack over one shoulder and put her hand on the stair rail, quickly snapping it back—the shiny metal balustrade burning her fingertips with residual heat.

'Sorry. Forgot to mention that.' The air steward smiled apologetically. 'There isn't much shade out there today. Actually, there's never really any shade out there,' she chuckled.

'All good.' Jenny returned the smile and carefully made her way down the aluminium mesh stairs, avoiding touching the railing again.

The tarmac radiated a heat haze, framed by hundreds of white dirt mounds as far as the eye could see. She'd studied them as the aircraft circled around making its final approach to the short runway.

Coober Pedy was said to have gotten its name from the local indigenous people who, after the opal mining boom in the early 1900's called it Kupa Piti, which meant 'white man's hole.' Jenny giggled silently at how strange it must have been to the aboriginal people to see hundreds of men swarm to the area to dig hole after hole and burrow their way to wealth.

Fluorescent orange triangle-rope lined the path on the tarmac, guiding the way to a small terminal that reminded her of an old transportable school building, complete with sash windows and bitumen cladding.

Opening the door to a wave of cool air, Jenny stopped a moment to savour it, knowing such luxury wouldn't last long. There was no baggage carousel and only two service counters, a few chairs and a vending machine in the far corner.

'Constable Williams?' Jenny turned to find a police officer strolling into the terminal from the other side. He was medium height, blonde, tanned and wore the khaki police uniform that was often issued in rural parts of Australia. Like the soldiers in the desert, it was cooler than the dark navy blue she'd been wearing since she joined the force after leaving school.

'That's me.'

'Your baggage won't take long.' He stepped forward, his hand offered in greeting. 'I'm Constable Philips. Welcome to Coober Pedy, the hottest, driest place on the continent.'

'So they tell me.'

'And you still came?' Jenny didn't get a chance to answer before Constable Philips was intercepting the luggage which was piled unceremoniously on top of a trailer, pulling up outside the tiny terminal. 'Which one is yours?'

'I'm good Constable Philips. I can carry my own bags.'

'Of course you can, but that wouldn't be polite. You're in the bush now Williams. You're gonna have to leave that city thinking behind.'

Jenny almost laughed out loud. 'I grew up on a dairy farm Philips. I'm hardly a fragile city girl, but I appreciate the country hospitality. Thanks. Mine is the cheap brown and tan bag that looks like it came from the two-dollar store.'

He nodded and headed out the back door, pointing out the bag to the baggage handler who probably moonlighted in an opal mine. His beard was long and shaggy and what skin wasn't covered by his long-sleeved cotton shirt and full-length pants was nearly as white as the zinc cream he'd applied to his nose to protect him from the scorching sun.

'Do I get to go to my accommodation before the station?' she asked Philips as he returned with her bag.

'Afraid not. Sarge wants to meet you first thing.'

'Let me guess. He wants to know if I'm up to the job so he can put me back on the plane before it leaves if I'm not.' Sergeant Mackenzie's reputation preceded him. Her station sergeant in Victor Harbor, where she was posted since her graduation, warned her he was a hard-nosed, old-school chauvinist.

'He's not that bad, but he'll be sussing you out for sure. We've never had a female officer volunteering to be stuck out here before. You saw the Gibber Plains when you flew over them right?' Jenny nodded as Philips opened the back of the white police Landcruiser and threw her bag in.

'Those shale-like rocks go on like the Sahara and we get less than six inches of rain in these parts, usually all in the same friggin' week, flooding the place out.'

'You're not selling it mate.'

'Sorry, but it's the truth and I guess that's why we don't get girls out here.'

'Well I'm not your average girl Philips.' And she wasn't. She'd grown up knee-deep in cow shit, riding horses, herding cows on motorbikes, driving tractors and ploughing paddocks. She'd held cow entrails in her hands while the vet operated on the animal, still awake and standing upright. There wasn't much that was going to phase her, except maybe this bloody heat.

But she hadn't volunteered to come to Coober Pedy to prove herself. The reason she'd come all this way, and was willing to stick it out in this God-forsaken place was personal and she wasn't about to share that reason with anyone—at least not yet.

Chapter 2

Constable Philips entered the station, moving toward the back office, but stopping short.

'I'll give her two weeks, a month tops. Once she meets a few of the locals, she'll high-tail it back to the city in a flash.'

'Come on Sarge, at least give her a go before you shoot her down.'

Philips cleared his throat as Jenny came up behind him.

From her position, in the front office just behind Philips, she could see her new commanding officer sitting behind his desk, his feet up on the corner as he leant back, hands behind his head. Across from him stood a tall, lanky looking man with thick dark hair, peppered with grey.

Both men turned toward the warning Philips gave them. Jenny failed to hear what the Sergeant said, but she hadn't missed the other officer's reply. They watched her carefully as she entered the back office.

'This is Constable Williams. Williams, this is Sergeant Mackenzie and Senior Constable O'Connell.'

'Pleased to meet you Williams.' O'Connell offered his hand in greeting. The Sergeant remained seated, his eyes moving up and down Jenny's body making her adjust her stance self-consciously. Annoyed with herself, she tried to ignore his steely grey eyes, probing her as though he could see inside her very soul.

He nodded for O'Connell to leave. The Senior Constable obliged, tapping Philips on the shoulder as he exited the office. Philips hesitated, as though he were about to say something, then turned and left.

'So Williams. How was your trip up?' Sergeant Mackenzie indicated for her to take a seat. For some reason, moving was a difficult task, her limbs heavy and a rising sense of unexpected anxiety. She should have been prepared for this scrutiny, after all, being female meant it wasn't anything new. The first few years in the Victor station were the same. Proving herself went with the territory. Her gender may or may not have been the issue—she knew all new officers needed to earn their stripes.

Finally, she lowered herself into the chair, which squeaked as her weight settled into it. 'It's only a few hours Sir. Amazing scenery flying in though.'

'Amazing isn't exactly how I'd describe it, but each to their own!'

'How long have you been here Sir, if you don't mind me asking?' He watched her with that penetrating gaze a moment, then nodded as if he'd answered an internal question.

'Twenty years Williams, so I've seen it all—you understand!' It wasn't a question; it was a warning.

'Perfectly Sir.'

'You keep your head down. Do as your told. Don't get any delusions of grandeur and you and I will get along just fine.'

Jenny frowned. 'Coober Pedy hasn't got any crime then Sir?'

He laughed, a deep, throaty laugh and Jenny continued to frown. 'Just petty stuff. Bar fights, arguments over mining claims from time to time and occasionally some idiot falls down a mine shaft in the dead of night and the State Emergency Service team have to spend days trying to find the dickhead, but apart from that, there isn't much to concern your pretty head about.'

'So four unsolved murders don't bother you?'

Sergeant Mackenzie's expression changed with an almost sinister grin that failed to reach his eyes. 'Now I understand why you took this placement. You're hoping to blaze a trail, make your mark and get yourself a promotion back in the big smoke. This isn't my first rodeo Williams. I've seen young constables like you come and go.'

'And how long do you give me Sarge?' There was no endearment in the term she used and her commanding officer didn't miss the tone.

'Don't test me Williams.'

'Wouldn't dream of it Sir. Can I go and unpack, get changed? When does my shift start?'

'We all work day shift here Williams. We all work night shift when we need to. Get dressed and get your arse back here before lunch.'

Jenny pushed to her feet, saluted and turned around on her heel as though she were on the parade ground, before marching from the office. She strode through the main office, where Philips met her, guiding her out the door, and collecting her suitcase as they exited.

'Well he's an arsehole.'

Philips grinned. 'Keep that opinion to yourself Williams. He's a good Sergeant. A little old-fashioned, but he gets the job done.'

'Archaic might be a better term.' She decided to change the subject. 'Where am I staying?'

'At the Opal Miner's Motel, just across the road.'

'Handy. Is it air-conditioned?'

'Yep and the town pool is just up the road so you can take a dip after a hot day on the job.'

'Sounds good.' Sweat ran down her back, soaking into her travel clothes. Maybe accepting the transfer in January wasn't the wisest idea. 'Sarge said you don't have much in the way of crime in Coober Pedy, but I've read the stats. That's not exactly true, is it?'

'It's isolated out here. People get a bit stir crazy at times. Stuff happens.'

'Stuff. Like a mother and daughter going missing, presumed murdered, likely by a local.' Philips stared at Jenny, his mouth open, his brow creased. Shaking his head, he shifted his gaze to the woman behind the desk in the motel reception.

'Marj. This is Jenny, Constable Williams, our newest addition.'

'Oh luv. You're too pretty to be hanging around with these rough lads.' Jenny relaxed and let her meeting with her commanding officer slide to the back of her mind. 'Here's your key luv. Danny, can you take her up and show her around?'

He hesitated a moment, but then Jenny saw she'd piqued his interest with her question about the missing persons case. He agreed with a nod and waved his hand for her to head out the door on the other side of the office.

'Thanks Marj.' Jenny waved as she left. 'Lovely to meet you.'

'You too luv. See you tonight.'

'Why did you ask about a missing mum and daughter case? That's a cold case from before my time. We have no new leads. Did someone send you up here to make sure we didn't miss anything?'

Philips stopped outside her door. The number two on the room number twelve hung upside down by one screw. She watched as Philips visibly fought the urge to put it right.

'Why would anyone want to send a constable with a few years of experience here to follow up on *your* case?' Jenny opened the door to the room and entered a narrow hall that led past the bathroom to the bedroom beyond. There was no kitchen, just coffee making facilities and a bar fridge.

Philips shrugged as if suddenly realising he should let the subject drop.

'Is there something more you're not telling me?' Jenny tossed the keys on the bed and turned back to search Philips' face.

He hesitated, then placed the bag inside the door and stepped back out of the room. 'See you back at the station.' He forced a smile then jogged off back towards work.

Jenny shut the door behind him with a sigh. Sliding the security bolt across, she picked up her bag and placed it on the bed, which absorbed the weight like a trampoline. The orange bedspread was a few decades too old, but the furniture was in good condition.

She opened the case and unpacked her new khaki uniform. Opening the hat box, she pulled out her Akubra style hat, putting it on her head before turning to see her reflection in the mirror over the dressing table.

She pulled the hat back off, tossing it gently to the bed then retrieved a manila folder from her suitcase and placed it on the dressing table. Reading the postcard again, she studied the picture of a rusty drilling truck. The tourist sign that marked Coober Pedy stared back at her. She flipped it over and read the hand-written message before placing it back in the folder.

Removing the photo of a woman from the file, she touched the face, then pressed it into the frame of the mirror. The second photo was of a teenager. This one she placed below the first and stopped to study them a moment. Her heart thudded in her chest, as though it were being physically torn to pieces. She shook herself free of the surging emotions.

'I promise I'll find you. One way or another, I'll get to the bottom of this.'

Chapter 3

Jenny entered the station to find Philips on the phone in the reception area and O'Connell at a small desk to the side, eyes focussed on an ancient computer screen.

She waved to Philips who waved back, then lifted the counter-top that separated the public from the officers and entered the staff only area.

'What do I need to do?'

'I think Philips might have a call out. You can go with him. He can show you around town a bit.' O'Connell hadn't taken his eyes off the screen.

'What you working on? Anything I can help with?'

'No, just filing a report. Lost property.'

'Really? What did you find?'

'Just an old calico bag with a few souvenirs in it. Some tourist or backpacker must have forgotten it.'

'Have they left town?'

'Probably. If no one claims it, we'll add it to the police charity auction at the end of the year.'

'Can I put it away for you?' Jenny could see the well-worn bag on the desk. She tentatively picked it up to look inside.

'Sure. There's a locker out the back we keep small stuff in. The key is hanging up there, with the blue tag.' O'Connell finally took his eyes from the screen.

Jenny tipped the contents out on the desk. There was a postcard with a print date of June 2001. 'This is a pretty old card.'

'They print them by the thousands. They last for decades.'

'Really?' Jenny began putting the items back in the bag.

'There's been an accident out by Ryan's field.' Philips hung up.

'Take Williams.'

'Yes Sir. You ready Williams? First call out.' He grinned with excitement that she didn't share.

'Let's do it.' Jenny put the calico bag on O'Connell's desk. 'I'll need a utility vest and a weapon.'

Philips strolled to a bank of lockers that lined the side wall alongside O'Connell's desk. 'In here.' He handed her a vest, already equipped with a Taser. 'It's probably a bit big, but we can get one altered to suit you later. Weapons are in the gun safe over there.' He pointed. 'Don't forget to log the serial number and sign for it.'

'What kind of accident?' Jenny put the vest on, grabbed a waist belt for her pistol and signed out her service weapon, before following Philips out the door.

'Not sure exactly. The S.E.S. are meeting us out there, but it sounds like old man Pickard has stumbled down a mineshaft while night fossicking.' They hopped into the Landcruiser and Philips started the engine.

'Night fossicking?'

'Yeah. Not everyone who mines has a legitimate claim. Pickard tends to like to play in the grey area. He takes a black light out at night and wanders around trying to find small opals in the discarded piles around the mines.'

'And that isn't legal?'

'Like I said, it's a grey area. He's fossicking, not mining, so it's not officially covered by the law and he doesn't need a claim. It's often called noodling, and it's usually done in the day light, because doing it at night is dangerous, but easier to spot the opals after dark with a black light. While noodling isn't illegal, doing it at night is down-right stupid and can be considered reckless endangerment, so can be an unlawful offence.'

'Oh.'

A dust cloud followed them as they left the station. Jenny spotted lights in the side mirror through the clouds of red that floated behind their vehicle. They pulled up seconds before the ambulance. The State Emergency Service were already on scene with a man in a harness being lowered under a tripod, a rescue stretcher attached.

'Seen anything yet?' Philips asked as he slammed the door of the Landcruiser.

'Not yet.' A stocky S.E.S volunteer peered into the darkness as his mate disappeared from sight.

Jenny surveyed the area, bordered by a sea of white dirt mounds and barren of anything green.

'How do you know he's down there then?' She approached, then stopped as stones rolled into the hole, throwing her off balance.

'Be careful there luv.' the S.E.S. worker offered with a smile.

'Williams, this is Frank. Frank, meet our newest addition, Constable Williams.'

'Nice to meet you. I'd offer to shake your hand, but mine are full.' Jenny watched as Frank used his hands to control the belay device as he slowly allowed his companion to descend into the mine safely.

'How do you know Pickard is down there?' she asked again.

'Someone passing by heard him calling out and reported it,' Philips offered.

'Oh you could have told me that earlier.' She slapped his arm lightly.

He grinned. 'Where's the fun in that?'

'Found him.' A call came from the depths of the pit. 'I'll need some help to load him in the stretcher.'

Jenny stepped back and watched the rescue operation unfolding. The S.E.S team worked with precision, like they'd done this a hundred times. Maybe they had. Apparently falling down the mine shafts wasn't uncommon. There were enough signs everywhere to warn against it, so it must have occurred with regularity.

'Hey, there's something else down here you're gonna want to see Philips.'

The S.E.S worker hung over his patient as they were winched to the surface. The paramedics rushed in, retrieved the stretcher and carried Pickard to the ambulance with the help of two S.E.S workers.

'What you got Geoff?' Philips stepped closer to the mine, his brow creased.

'A pile of bones.'

'Probably a dingo.'

'Nah mate. It's a sack of bones covered in clothing. Woman's clothing.' He pulled a pack of tobacco from inside his bright orange overalls and began rolling up a smoke as he perched casually on the side of the mine—still hanging on his safety line.

'Can I take a look?' The faces in her photos popped into Jenny's head.

'No, you go with Pickard to the hospital. Get his statement. I'll check this out.' Jenny glanced over her shoulder as the paramedic did obs on Pickard before taking him to Emergency.

'Do you have a forensic unit here?'

Philips laughed. 'No. But if the remains are human, we'll call in the big guns from Adelaide.'

Jenny hopped from one foot to the other, desperate to get down and see the body—to find out if it was one of the women she was looking for—but she'd only just arrived and there was no way she was going to be able to take lead on this one.

'Maybe call O'Connell in first.' The ambulance rear doors closed with a thud.

'I've got this Williams.' Philips didn't hide his agitation.

'Okay. I'm sorry. You're right. I'll follow Pickard to the hospital. She waved for the paramedics to wait for her. As she rushed toward the ambulance, she caught Philips' reply.

'You do that.'

Chapter 4

'Can I ask him questions?' Jenny sat in the ambulance as the paramedic placed an IV in Mr Pickard's arm.

'You've got a few minutes before the pethidine starts to take effect.'

'Okay, thanks.' Jenny shuffled closer to the patient and pulled her mobile phone from her pocket, ready to take notes. 'Mr Pickard.'

'Call me Rick sweetheart.' The filthy-tooth grin stopped Jenny from finding the endearment offensive. She'd worked hard to become a police officer and even harder to be taken seriously in the male dominated world. Thankfully times were changing and old guys like Rick didn't mean anything but good intentions with their old-school references. Not like her new boss.

'Okay, Rick. When did you fall down the shaft?'

'I don't know exactly but after midnight.'

'Did you see anything in the shaft?'

'It was pitch black *sweetheart*.' Okay, that time it might have been used a little sardonically. 'I couldn't see me hand in front of me face until the sun started to come up this morning. By then, the pain in me leg was killing me that much I was nearly passing out.'

Damn, she'd hoped to find out more about the body in the shaft.

'Did you fall, or were you pushed?'

'Just fell darlin'.' Another endearment. 'I'm a stumbling old fool these days, but I make me livin' doing what I do, so, well, it is what it is.' There was a moment of silence. 'You're new round here.' His words were starting to slur as the pethidine took effect.

'Yes Mr.. Rick. It's my first day.'

'Glad I could…welcome you… then.' His eyes closed. Jenny turned to the paramedic.

'He's out for the count. I'm guessing he's been awake all night and in pain.

'How long will he be out?'

'Can't be sure. Pethidine is different for each patient, but if you hang around or come back after the doctors have checked him out, you'll be able to ask him more questions.'

The ambulance pulled up outside the Emergency Department of the small, remote hospital. Jenny rose, ready to climb out as the orderly opened the rear door. 'Thanks. I'll check in at the station and get back to you.'

She jumped down, then swung around to leave, almost bumping into a man in a white coat, his stethoscope swinging around his neck. 'Oh sorry.' She peered into almost black eyes that twinkled with mirth. 'I'm still getting…' she lost her train of thought a moment, 'my bearings.'

'You must be the new Constable.' The doctor's eyes were smiling at her and his voice sounded melodically as he greeted her. 'Can't stop to chat. I'll see you tonight then.'

The Doctor indicated for the orderly to take the patient inside and scooted off after the gurney without further explanation.

Jenny frowned, put her phone back in her pocket and stared as the team disappeared behind the Emergency Department doors.

'See you tonight.' The paramedic repeated the same phrase as he jumped into the passenger's seat of the ambulance and it drove off.

Jenny stared at the retreating ambulance, her mouth open, shaking her head. What just happened? Brushing off the strange comments, she headed out from under the emergency entrance into the hot sun. Sweat started to run down her back before she took a dozen steps toward the police station. There was no doubt in her mind it was going to be a long, hot summer.

Any hopes of finding shade on the way were dashed as Jenny continued walking down McDougal Road. Dark, wet stains appeared under her arms, her sports bra was soaked. Stopping, she considered her surroundings. The pebbled roadside was devoid of even a blade of grass or salt bush. The heat coming off one of the few bitumen roads in town was stifling. The realisation she had no idea where the station was made her reassess her plans.

She retrieved her mobile phone from her front pocket and pulled up her map app, tapping in the hospital to get an idea of how far away she was from the station. In front of her she could see mining equipment on the hill, surrounded by endless piles of discarded white dirt.

The terrain reminded her of a moonscape—barren and damn right inhospitable. But she was there for more than a career move. She wanted answers and she wasn't going to get them whinging about the heat or the long walk back to the station.

'No way!' she said aloud as she asked her map app how far from the hospital to the station. Twenty-two bloody minutes on foot. That wasn't even close to a smart move in this heat. It must have been close to thirty-eight degrees Celsius already, and nearly the hottest part of the day.

Sucking in a deep breath, she returned to the shade, her phone to her ear as she waited for someone to pick up.

'Coober Pedy Police.'

'It's Constable Williams. I'm at the hospital. Any chance one of you guys can call by and pick me up?'

'I'm not your bloody chauffeur Williams. Why aren't you with Philips?'

'I was Sir.' She wasn't sure if she was speaking with O'Connell or the Sergeant, but either way, they were her superior. Despite their Scottish and Irish names, the Senior Constable and the Sergeant had thick, country Aussie accents and she was still getting used to which was which. 'Until Philips asked me to ride with Mr Pickard back to the hospital and ask him a few questions, while he investigated the body in the mine shaft.'

'Alright. I'm on my way out to the site now so I'll swing by and pick you up on the way.'

'Thank you Sir. I'll wait outside Emergency.'

'Be there in ten minutes.'

Chapter 5

'Any word on who the body is Sir?' Jenny put on her seatbelt as Senior Constable O'Connell put his pedal to the metal, forcing her back in the bucket seat. Jenny fought the urge to put her fingernails through the seat to brace herself.

'We have to leave her where she is for now, but she wasn't in any recognisable shape. Just a skeleton.'

Jenny watched the dust cloud in the side mirror as it billowed and hung in the still air, leaving a fog of red behind them.

'Why leave her there though?' O'Connell took a hard right, the wheels sliding on the loose road surface. Jenny grabbed the handle above the side window to keep herself seated, wondering what the emergency might be, the woman was already dead.

'Philips went in the hole after you left and he can't be sure she died from the fall, so we need to call in a forensic unit from the big smoke. They are putting someone on a plane as we speak. They should be here by mid-afternoon.'

'So once the body is recovered, we'll be sifting dirt for evidence then?'

'Looks like it.' The accident site came into view and O'Connell almost did a handbrake slide as they stopped beyond the now taped off area.

'Senior.' Philips met them at the vehicle. 'I've left everything like you said, waiting on forensics, but I did take a look for any ID, as much as I could without disturbing the scene. Found this.' Jenny was surprised to see him pull up a photo on his mobile phone. Philips was about two years older than Jenny, but she thought years in the bush might have slowed down his adoption of technology. It seemed she was wrong.

'Tiffany. That's Tiffany down there?' O'Connell rubbed his chin. 'Mark said she left him to go back to the city. Couldn't hack living below ground he said.'

'That's what he told me too. I was talking to him in the pub a few months back. Got himself another girlfriend, but it didn't last long.'

'Take Williams, have a little chat with Mark and see when he last saw Tiffany. I'll finish up here and meet the forensic scientist at the airport when he arrives.'

'Will do Sir. Williams.' Philips ushered her toward his vehicle.

'So Tiffany was a local?'

'If that's her, then yep.'

'And her boyfriend said she left town?'

'Yep, that's what he told me. We'll go have a chat with him now. See what's up.' Philips opened the car door and got in behind the wheel.

'You can't tell him you think she's dead though.' Jenny did her seatbelt up, but didn't take her eyes from Philips as he put his key in the ignition.

'Why not?' Philips started the car and backed up toward the dirt track leading to town.

'Because he never reported her missing and we don't know she's dead yet, just someone with her ID is.'

Philips nodded as he turned left, heading North. 'I suppose you're right.'

'Just an outsider's perspective maybe. Have you checked to see if anyone ever reported Tiffany missing?'

'You training for the Criminal Investigation Branch or something? If not, you probably should be. Give the station a call now and find out.'

Jenny began to dial. 'How long have you known this guy?'

'Twenty years.' Jenny controlled her emotions as she wondered how on earth a country cop was going to remain objective when they'd grown up with someone who could be a suspect in a suspicious death?

'Sir. Just wondering if you can check something for us. O'Connell is still on site and we need to interview Mark...' Jenny glanced at Philips.

'Nesbitt.' Philips offered.

'Mark Nesbitt about Tiffany's disappearance but we don't want to tip him off her body might have been found.'

'Good call.' Sarge sounded surprised. 'What do you need?'

'Can you see if anyone reported Tiffany missing— parents, brother, sister, friend? Anyone?'

'I'll run it through the computer and send you a text, but if they did, I never heard about it.'

'Thank you Sir.' Jenny hung up and put her phone back in her pocket, wondering why no one might have reported her missing.

'How long have you been a cop in Coober Pedy then?'

'Since I graduated, nearly seven years now.'

'I thought the community here was mostly transient?'

'Some are, but we have a core of locals, who've grown up here or moved here years ago to try their hand at opal mining and just never left. Like Marj.'

'What's her story then?' Jenny surveyed the landscape as they drove along another dirt track. The sun belted down on the vehicle, the air-conditioning next to useless. She resisted the urge to pull her shirt away from her sweating underarms.

'You'll have to ask her. She tells it so much better than I can.' Jenny frowned. 'Really! It's a great story. She'll tell you tonight if you ask.'

'About that? What's with the Doctor and the Paramedic asking....'

'Here we are.'

Jenny turned in her seat, taking in the barren mounds of rubble and slightly undulating landscape. 'There's only dirt here.' All thought of asking the question that was on the tip of her tongue moments ago disappeared as she searched for Mark Nesbitt's home.

'It's like Tatooine.'

'Like what?'

'Star Wars. Tatooine. Luke Skywalker's home, in the desert except we don't farm moisture, we mine opals.' He opened the door and got out. Jenny watched him move toward a large outcrop of stone, her mouth open as she tried to get her head around the Star Wars reference.

Philips stopped, turned and waved for her to follow him. She watched through the windscreen a moment, shook her head and opened the door to get out.

'What on earth are you on about?' she asked as she caught up with a quick jog, sweat now running down her back making her regret the exertion. Going for a jog for fitness in this place was going to have to happen after dark, if at all. The heat was brutal.

'It's easier to show you.' He walked up a slight incline. 'Not a Star Wars fan then?'

'Not really.'

'My dad would say that was sacrilege. We grew up on it. I saw the remastered versions in the cinema in Adelaide for my tenth birthday. I used to watch it on VHS video replay over and over when I was little, until DVD's came out.' They reached the sandstone monolith and Philips stopped, blushing as he realised he'd been waffling on. 'Sorry about that.'

'No, it's interesting. I grew up on a dairy farm. My dad was too busy trying to make a living to take me to the movies but we did have a video player.'

'More the Disney movie type?'

'Not on your life. I'm a Noir crime lover and horror movie fan. I've watched every Christopher Lee movie ever released and Dial M for Murder is my all-time favourite Noir crime, well that and Key Largo. Who doesn't love a Bogart film?'

Philips laughed. 'No wonder you decided to become a cop.' He knocked on a wooden door that resembled a barn gate from an old Mexican film. 'Mark. It's Danny. You in there mate?'

'Coming.' The door opened with a creak after a few seconds. 'Danny. I wasn't expecting anyone.'

'All good. I know the reception is crap out here. I was just out this way on a case and wanted to ask you a few questions about Tiffany.'

Mark frowned a moment, then opened the door wider. 'Who's your friend?' His eyes roamed Jenny's body from top to toe.

'This is Constable Williams, just arrived in town.'

'Literally.' Jenny offered her hand in greeting as she stepped into the window-less home. Wires ran around the wall to power switches sitting proud on stone walls. An old nineteen fifties kitchen sink stood alongside a lonely four burner electric stove against the far wall. An assortment of op-shop furniture occupied the living area.

'Not as bright and airy as Luke Skywalker's place,' she whispered and Philips chuckled under his breath. She'd seen Star Wars, once, while at a friend's house and this place didn't come close to resembling the underground home in Tatooine. This was dark, so dark her eyes needed time to adjust.

'Is my love-life really something that requires questioning?' Mark plonked down on the lounge closest to the kitchen sink, while Philips took the single, threadbare chair opposite. Jenny remained standing, taking in the rough walls, cut out of the sandstone and painted. She could see the tool marks under the paintwork and peered down a darkened tunnel as her interest piqued.

She'd heard about the Dugouts that many miners in Coober Pedy cut out of the earth while searching for opals. She planned on visiting some of the few open to tourists and hoped they were more impressive than this one. Sure, they were basically caves, with tunnels burrowed deep into the earth, but she'd expected so much more than what Mark's place offered.

'It's a police matter mate. We have a line of enquiry that says Tiffany never made it home.'

'That's because she took off with another bloke.'

'Really. You never mentioned it.'

Mark shrugged. 'A bit embarrassing isn't it? We were together over a year. I thought we were going good, but she said she'd hooked up with someone else and was leaving.'

Jenny resisted the urge to point out the obvious—that living in squalor like this dark and dingy hole in the earth wasn't exactly living the dream, but she stayed silent.

'What's this all about anyway? Tiffany didn't have much in the way of family, so who reported that she didn't get home?'

'It's an ongoing investigation. Did Tiffany ever tell you more about the guy?'

'Nope. Why would she? One minute she was here, the next, she says she's leaving with some rich guy and then she's out the door.'

24

'Anyone she'd confide in, in town?' Jenny asked, her butt leaning against the stainless-steel sink, full of unwashed dishes.

'Cheryl maybe.'

'Cheryl?'

'That would be Cheryl Peterson,' Philips said. 'Thanks Mark. We'll let you know if we have any more questions.' He got up from the chair, checked his hands a moment before wiping them on his trousers. He gave a nod to Jenny that it was time to leave.

'Is she alright?' Mark got up as Philips made his way to the door.

'You'll be the first to know if she isn't mate, promise.'

Chapter 6

'We should wait for an ID before we interview Cheryl.'

'You're probably right.' The two constables entered the station. Jenny stopped in front of the old window mounted air-conditioning unit, barely resisting the urge to lift her shirt and dry out the sweat that was running under her bra band.

'Bit warm for you Williams?' Sarge manned the front counter, the only officer left with them all out and about.

'Get anything on a missing person report for Tiffany?' Jenny decided not to make the smart-arsed remark that she hadn't spent the day on her butt in the air-conditioning like him.

'There is no report. I didn't think there would be. I've been here for twenty years. I'd have known if we needed to investigate a missing person in Coober Pedy.'

Jenny wondered why he hadn't found anything about her missing persons, but once more bit her lip to keep quiet.

'Something on your mind Williams?' Her expression must have given her away. Maybe she wasn't as smart as she thought she was. Time to practise the poker face in the mirror.

'Just thinking.' That used to always work with her mum.

'Mark said Tiffany took off with a guy, loaded with cash he says, but who knows.' Philips put the car keys on the hook behind the counter and poured a cup of water from the water cooler. 'Want one?'

'Yes please.' Jenny joined him. 'Until we confirm the body is Tiffany's there isn't much point chasing down who she might or might not have left town with.'

'That's tomorrow's job.' O'Connell entered the foyer. A tall, broad shouldered woman around Jenny's age sauntered in alongside. They carried large black bags, and O'Connell held a metal box that reminded Jenny of her dad's dented and chipped tool chest back on the farm.

'This is Penny, she's our forensic crime scene investigator.'

'Hey.' Penny put her case down and shook Jenny's hand, then Philips'. She gave Sarge a quick salute before picking up her bag once more. 'Can we get started this afternoon?'

'It's the hottest part of the day right now. I think, if it's alright with you, we'll pick this up at six a.m.' O'Connell checked his watch. 'I'll drop you off at the motel, then we can all meet at the front bar after.' It didn't sound like the bar was an option. Penny raised an eyebrow, implying Jenny, as a fellow female officer might have an answer. But she didn't have any idea what was going on.

'I'll show her Sir.' Jenny offered and O'Connell nodded.

'Leave all your forensic kit here, just take your luggage. We'll pick it all up in the morning before we head out.'

'Okay, sounds good.' Penny put her black bag down behind the counter and slung her duffle bag over her shoulder. 'Right to go then.'

Jenny led the way out the front door.

'What was that all about?' Penny asked as soon as they were out of earshot.

'No idea. This is my first day in town. Seems like beer o'clock comes early in the bush.'

'Seems that way.' They crossed the narrow bitumen road and headed over to the motel and caravan park. The red sand covered Jenny's shoes and it was only day one. She couldn't help but wonder how much dirt would be caked on them by the end of the week.

27

'I didn't expect to catch a murder on day one.'

'Saves the boredom.' They reached the reception area.

'Hi Marj. This is Penny. She's with the Forensic lab in Adelaide. Did one of the boys at the station book her a room?'

'They certainly did luv. Forensic lab hey.' Marj reached for a set of keys on a numbered hook behind the desk, one eye still on Penny. 'That's exciting. Heard they found a mass grave under old Pickard in the mine today.'

Jenny chuckled. 'Who told you that Marj?'

'You're not denying it then?'

'Nothing like that, I assure you.'

'Then why the forensic lady?' Marj hooked her head at Penny, one eyebrow raised.

'We found something that needs checking out. Just routine.' Jenny played the issue down.

'You can't fool me luv. I've lived in this place for thirty-five years and I've only seen forensic scientists and major crime detectives here five times, including today.'

'Thirty-five years, interesting. I might have a few questions for you later.' The rounded redhead seemed surprised.

'Like what?'

'Like how did you end up here thirty-five years ago?' All thought of the case was lost as she handed the key for room five to Penny and grinned wickedly.

'Oh, that *is* a good story. Did Danny tell you about it?'

'No. Absolutely not. He told me I needed to wait for you to tell the story because apparently, it's a doozy.'

'It is luv. I'll tell you tonight. See you in the bar soon.'

'What's with the bar and everyone telling me they'll see me tonight?'

'You'll see.' Marj grinned cheekily. 'Take Penny to freshen up and put on something nice. It's not often we get new girls in town and the fellas with be hanging around like bar flies.'

Jenny glanced at Penny, the same mix of confusion and suspicion running through her head was mirrored on her new friend's face.

'You're not setting me up on my first night are you Marj?' Jenny waggled her finger at the woman who feigned ignorance with a dramatic hand to her chest.

'Just get cleaned up and grab a beer at the bar when you're ready. First one is on the house, for both of you.'

Jenny led the way from reception, stopping in front of room five.

'Now none of that sounds suspicious at all!' Penny joked as she put the key in the door and turned. A wave of cool air greeted them as she opened it. 'Oh that is glorious.'

'It is.' Jenny leant against the doorframe, allowing the moisture to evaporate from her face. 'I don't know what's going on, but a paramedic and a doctor at the hospital both said 'see you tonight', so I'm thinking either Marj has told the whole town I'm a single female or it's just welcome drinks for the newbie.'

'Either way, we get a drink on the house. I'll tidy myself up and see you in the bar.'

'See you then.' Jenny pulled the door shut and started down the covered walkway to her room. She hadn't left the air-conditioner on all day, but the room was still cooler than outside. O'Connell was right, late afternoon was sweltering and no one in their right mind would be out causing trouble in this heat. It would be far more likely to get lively after dark in this town.

She put her keys on the dresser and studied the two faces staring back at her. Melanie was her cousin. As kids, they'd been inseparable. Her uncle Peter shared ownership of her family dairy farm which had two old farm houses, a large rotary dairy and five-hundred acres of prime grassland. She could almost smell the irrigated Lucerne now.

When she wasn't at school, or helping on the farm, she was over at Melanie's or Melanie over at her place or they'd be horseriding or motorbike riding or doing whatever silly teenage girls did together.

Then her aunt and Melanie had gone on a trip. Apparently, Aunt Carolyn wanted a holiday, and Melanie finishing year twelve a good excuse. At least that's what uncle Pete said. But even as a teenager Jenny was aware their marriage wasn't all roses.

Melanie used to regularly offload about their fighting, but it was just the usual things that happened in some relationships as people grew apart. The dairy industry was tough going back then, with milk prices not being any higher than they'd been decades before and costs rising, interest rates skyrocketing. It was a difficult time.

Aunt Carolyn and Melanie never made it home and all Jenny had to go on was the postcard she'd gotten from Coober Pedy, nine years ago.

She shook herself from her melancholy and turned to open her suitcase, still sitting full of clothing on her bed. She placed her cosmetics bag aside, before throwing clothing in various piles over the bedspread, seeking something decent to wear.

She'd packed enough clothing to last a week while the rest of her personal effects came up via a courier, but she hadn't anticipated a night on the town. Maybe she should have. It was time to lighten up a little. Her life had been a rollercoaster since that final year of school.

Police basic training, a few extra courses to specialise at the academy, then a year and a half as a probationary constable.

It took nearly five years of waiting for a placement in the Coober Pedy area to come up and when she'd jumped at it, her Sergeant had been sorry to see her leave.

Opening the wardrobe, she found a total of four coat hangers fixed to the railing. She took her spare uniform out and hung it first, wondering if there was an iron in the room, but decided there probably wasn't.

Next, she found her favourite peasant blouse, which she matched with a tailored pair of shorts. There were no pretty sandals or high heels to jazz up the outfit. All she possessed in that moment, other than her work shoes were the tattered edged sandshoes she'd worn on the plane.

She washed under her arms and dried before spraying on a healthy helping of deodorant. Finally, a bit of lipstick, mascara and blush finished off the look. She pulled her hair out of the ponytail and brushed it until it glowed. The only benefit of having thick, long hair was that other than putting it up, there was not much to getting it ready for a night out.

With one final look at Melanie and Carolyn's photos, she left, locking the door behind her.

As she stepped out, she saw Penny a few steps ahead and smiled to herself as she called out. 'I didn't think you'd be one to fuss around too much.'

Penny turned and gave a crooked grin. 'I'm already too gorgeous to need to do all that cosmetic crap.'

'How did you know to pack something to wear though?'

'I've been shipped here, there and everywhere to assess crime scenes and I know the bush boys love a good night on the town, just about any night of the week.'

'Well, my gear is still on the way up here, so this is it.' Jenny presented her outfit with her hand as if she were doing a magic trick.

'You look hot. You'll be beating them off with a stick in this place. I guarantee it.' Penny turned and carried on walking to the bar as Jenny caught up.

As she reached the entrance, the double glass doors opened like they were greeting royalty. Philips held one side, O'Connell the other, both with adolescent grins plastered in place.

'You win. I'll buy the first round.' O'Connell offered as they closed the doors behind the girls. Philips grinned but didn't elaborate and Jenny found no time to question what the bet was about.

'Over here ladies,' the barman called. 'Beer or wine?'

'I'll go a beer thanks.' Jenny sat down at the vinyl bar stool as a schooner of pale ale appeared.

'Girl after my own heart,' the barman smiled. 'And what about you luv?' He was about fifty years old, with suntanned skin and dark, almost black eyes. When he smiled all the lines around his eyes smiled with him and Jenny couldn't help but return the expression.

'I'll have a merlot if you have one, otherwise any red will do.'

'Merlot it is.'

The motel bar was already starting to fill and the feedback from a microphone brought about a number of complaints and thrown coasters at the man who wielded the mic like he would rather be just about anywhere else in the world.

Sergeant Mackenzie tapped the top of the microphone and was greeted with another round of feedback, followed by more cardboard coasters.

'Come on guys. Show a little respect.' The Sergeant puffed up his chest. 'Thanks for coming everyone.' He spoke into the microphone.

'Get on with it Sarge,' a few hecklers called.

The front door opened and Marj snuck in, followed closely by those deep brown eyes that caught Jenny off-guard at the hospital. The doctor gave her a wink as Sarge started speaking again.

'Well you all know we've been a man down for a few months at the station. Thankfully the big boys in town finally decided to spare us a little help.'

Jenny cringed as she realised this wasn't just a few welcome drinks. This was going to be a full-on meet and greet the whole flaming town.

'I know how much you local boys have been getting away with since Len left, but our newest team member, Constable Jenny Williams…' hoots and hollers including a few wolf whistles sounded as Sergeant Mackenzie shushed and waved his hand for calm.

'Constable Williams joins us from the seaside township of Victor Harbor. Holy hell, what a change.' He grinned, something not seen so far today. 'Constable Williams, why don't you come up here and introduce yourself?'

Jenny was sure she was going a deep shade of scarlet as she smiled politely and tried to decline but Marj grabbed her by the arm. 'Come on girl. Don't make us beg.' Jenny turned to Penny for support, not sure why, but hoping the woman might understand. Penny raised her glass in salute. Some help she was going to be.

Finally giving in, Jenny took the two steps to the small stage area at the back of the room and joined her new boss. As she stared out at the sea of faces before her, there was only one she focussed on – the doctor from Emergency, who was even more handsome in his denim shirt and moleskin trousers—standing at the back, leaning against the wall with his beer to his lips.

Chapter 7

Heat rushed to Jenny's cheeks as she awkwardly stepped down from the stage. Basic training had nothing on this. Marj handed her back her beer which she sculled quickly to dull her nerves.

Public speaking was never her strong point. She tried to recollect exactly what she'd said, but couldn't.

'Another round for the newbie.' The barman placed another beer on the bar in front of her as she arrived next to Penny.

'Well, that was entertaining.'

'I'm glad you think so.'

'Karaoke next. What's your singing voice like luv?' The barman wiped the highly-polished timber top down and tossed new cardboard coasters out to protect it.

'Jenny. I have a few people here I think you should meet, formally.' Marj dragged two men up, looking slightly less embarrassed than Jenny.

'This is Tim Burns. He's our Senior Paramedic and this is *Doctor* Nev Newman. I think you've met the lads today.'

'I did, thank you Marj.'

'Pleased to meet you Jenny. Welcome to Coober Pedy.' Jenny offered her hand to Tim, but he grabbed her around the shoulders in a brotherly bear hug. She would have returned the gesture, but her arms were pinned to her sides.

'Thanks Tim,' she stuttered as he physically shook the words out of her.

'Put her down, you don't know where she's been,' Penny teased.

'Oh, sorry.' He grinned sheepishly at Penny.

Jenny gazed from one to the other and frowned. 'Have you two met before?'

Penny shrugged. 'I've been out this way a couple of times for work, but Tim and I go way back.'

'Yeah, we went to uni together.'

'Nice.' Jenny took another sip of beer, the condensation dripping from the bottom of the glass, running down her hand.

'It's good to meet you Jenny.' Nev offered his hand. Jenny quickly wiped off the moisture and shook it, their touch lingering a moment. Nev's dark eyes almost glistened and Jenny was transfixed for a moment, before 'My achy breaky heart' screeched over the microphone and all heads spun round to see a local opal miner, still covered in dust from a full day underground, giving his rendition of Billy Ray Cyrus' one and only mainstream hit. Of course, country music enthusiasts would likely disagree.

'Oh my God. That is awful.' Jenny resisted the temptation to put her hands over her ears.

'That's John. He's our regular ice-breaker. Believe it or not, he gets better with more beer.' Nev grinned and a small dimple appeared on his chin.

'More beer for him or me?' Jenny took another swig.

'Probably the latter.' Nev leant in close to Jenny so she could hear him over the worst karaoke she'd ever known. The warmth of his breath and scent of his cologne made her skin tingle. She scolded herself. She wasn't here in the middle of nowhere to hook up. Staying focussed was her priority right now.

Nev must have sensed something, a frown appeared between his brown eyebrows. 'You into karaoke?' The frown was gone.

'Not on your life. There isn't enough beer in the whole town to get me drunk enough to get up there.'

'You want a refill Nev?' A short, busty woman in her mid-twenties collected the empty schooner glasses from the bar, her eyes lingering on the doctor.

'Thanks Cheryl. That would be good. What about you?' He waited for Jenny to judge her half-empty glass. She nodded. She'd take another.

'You're trying to get me up on that stage, aren't you?' Jenny teased and Nev laughed aloud as two more schooners of beer were heavily slammed down onto the towelling bar-runner which featured the various beer brands on offer.

Jenny frowned, her eyes scanning Nev then Cheryl, realisation hitting home. She was about to excuse herself, when Nev picked up the beers and turned toward her. 'Let's go find a table before the place fills up and we end up eating dinner off our lap.' Nev turned his back on Cheryl who huffed before another patron called out for service at the other end of the bar.

'We are grabbing a table, you good?' Jenny asked Penny who was deep in conversation with Tim.

'Sure,' she answered loudly, just as John finally finished screeching into the mic.

The four of them manoeuvred through the tables, making their way to a long table where Danny sat. Next to him a woman with a toddler on her lap, watched to see who the next karaoke contestant would be. There were still a few empty chairs. Nev approached Danny.

'You good if we sit here Dan?'

'No worries Nev.'

They sat and Danny tapped the woman next to him on the shoulder. He began to sign something and Jenny realised the woman must have been hearing impaired. 'This is our new Constable Jenny, Jenny, this is my wife Dianna and our son Tommy.' He spoke as his fingers signed with well-practised precision.

'Pleased to meet you.' Jenny made eye contact hoping Dianna could read lips. The woman smiled and signed to Danny.

'Lovely to meet you.' Danny translated before a few more words were signed without explanation. Jenny asked the question with her eyes and the two giggled happily.

'She said you are very beautiful for a cop.' The group at the table laughed and Jenny blushed. She never thought of herself as beautiful. Tall, lean on the edge of skinny with plain features, she'd been teased mercilessly at school. If it hadn't been for her cousin Melanie being in her grade, popular and willing to stick it to the bullies, her school life would have been miserable – Melanie always stuck up for her.

She pushed the thought away when she realised everyone was waiting on her response.

'Oh. Thanks.' She gazed into her beer, her finger made circles in the never-ending layers of condensation. The air-conditioning was struggling to keep up with the number of bodies in the bar and although it was much cooler than outside, it was still not cold by any stretch of the imagination.

'So, your first day has been eventful by the sound of it.' Nev scanned the faces around the table. Penny and Tim sat opposite, next to Dianna, her son squirming in her lap beginning to get bored with all the grown-ups.

'You can say that again. There's not been a body in years and Williams arrives, and wham, there one is. I hope it isn't a taste of things to come.' Danny's eyes studied Jenny. 'Did dead bodies turn up much where you were last stationed?'

'No. You can't put this one on me. Whoever she is, she's been dead a while. Just bones from all accounts. That's well before my time and influence.'

'We'll find out tomorrow. I'll be in that hole just after six.' Penny lifted her glass of wine. 'So let's toast to an early night, hey?'

'I don't think so. This is the bush Penny. Since when can you go to work early without a big night out on the town first?' Tim offered. 'You do remember last time you came to town?' A wide grin spread across his cheeks, highlighting his freckles that matched is auburn mop of hair.

Chapter 8

Jenny's eyes snapped open, her alarm blaring, the red numbers blurrily flashing 5.00. She threw her head back on the pillow, the throbbing behind her eyes and the tackiness of her tongue reminded her why she didn't usually drink much.

'For crying out loud.' She thumped the snooze button. The last thing she remembered was Nev, Penny and herself belting out *ABBA's Dancing Queen* after running through just about every hit the band ever made. How on earth did anyone convince her to get up on stage? She'd never live this down. The boys at the station would be all over it. She'd likely find photos pinned up throughout the break room or worse, somewhere Sarge could find them.

Luckily her boss had gone home before the messy part of the evening started. She'd forgotten just how hard med students partied. 'Should have known better,' she muttered. One small grace was she hadn't been drunk enough to end up in Nev's bed. She assumed, as much as she liked the idea, he was a bit of a lady's man judging by Cheryl's dirty looks— getting distracted wasn't in her plans. The last thing she wanted was to be killing time in Coober Pedy longer than necessary.

The snooze button didn't last. The return of its blaring siren reminded her there was somewhere she needed to be by six. Dragging herself out of bed, she stumbled into the shower. Water was at a premium in this isolated town with little or no rainfall, but she needed to wake herself up.

Turning on the cold tap, she relished the chill of the water as it flowed down her body, reinvigorating her inside and out. Her skin began to tingle, signalling it was time to get out. She quickly dried off, dragged a comb through her wet hair and pulled it back into a pony tail. Grabbing her only clean uniform, she dressed, thinking she'd need to make a quick visit to the laundry tonight or she'd have nothing to wear tomorrow.

Fully planning to be in the dining room early for breakfast, she was surprised to find it busy. It seemed the town started early to avoid the heat. By five-thirty, she was standing at the breakfast buffet trying to decide if it was wise to have a hot breakfast since she'd likely be skipping lunch.

Loading her plate with scrambled eggs, two miniature sausages and three rashers of bacon, before pouring a hot cup of drip-filtered coffee, she made it to her seat only to be joined by Penny a few minutes later.

'What time did you make it to bed?' she asked her new friend through a mouthful of toast.

'No idea, just after you and Nev left.'

'I left with Nev?' Jenny stopped chewing. That, she definitely didn't recall.

Penny laughed. 'You were too far gone for anything to have happened. Don't panic. I believe he just wanted to make sure you made it to your room before he went home.

'How embarrassing.'

'Don't be stupid. Everyone parties hard out here. Other than digging for opals, riding motorbikes or bush bashing, there isn't exactly much else to do.'

Jenny scoffed the rest of her breakfast without another word. Penny did the same as she studied the time and realised there were only ten more minutes left to get to the station.

'Time for a morning jog then?' Penny teased as they left the motel restaurant.

'I just ate a mountain of food, but maybe getting to work early is a good idea.' Jenny nodded, then took off at a jog as the sun rose over the Eastern opal fields.

'That is spectacular.' Penny stopped in front of the station, the doors closed, the lights still out.

Jenny watched as the sun slowly appeared. The town was just coming to life, with the sound of the occasional motor being booted into action. She knew that later in the day, all sorts of noises would ring out—like explosions as new areas of underground mine were blasted out, and machinery, especially blowers clearing away rubble and dirt, but for now it was peaceful, almost serene.

'Morning girls.' O'Connell arrived and unlocked the front door, leaning in and flicking a light switch on before holding the door for them.

'Morning Sir.' They answered in unison.

'Philips will be here any second. I'll get him to transport you out to the site.' He studied Jenny a moment. 'You could have kept your dirty uniform on from yesterday Williams because you are going to be stuck down the hole sifting dirt all day.'

Jenny sighed. 'All good Sir. Best to start the day looking respectable.'

'Fair enough. I like your attitude.' O'Connell followed them inside, flicking on more lights and firing up the two front office computers.

'How did you two pull up?' Philips was grinning mischievously as he entered.

'We're all good thanks.' Jenny offered, but Philips' face didn't change and she was now sure that photos would begin appearing by the time she got back later in the day.

'Ready to get going?'

'Ready as we'll ever be.'

'Did you bring water?'

'Shit.' Jenny huffed. 'My gear hasn't arrived and I still don't have my stainless-steel insulated water bottles.

'I've got a plastic ten litre water container in the back with a few cups. We'll be good but you might need something on you while you're in the hole. It's cooler below ground, but still hot and dirty work.'

'You've done this before?' Jenny asked as they made their way to the Landcruiser.

'A few times, but I used to mine here too. My dad owned a claim not far from where Pickard fell in.'

'How is he doing by the way? I should have asked Nev last night but totally forgot.'

'Good. Broken leg, otherwise unscathed. Did he have anything interesting to add to the investigation?' Jenny got in the passenger side as Penny jumped in the back.

'Only that he fell, in the night. Wasn't pushed. Didn't know the body was there.'

'That was my guess. Hopefully we can get some confirmation we have Tiffany down there so we can carry on finding out how and why she ended up in a disused mine.'

'And, hopefully a cause of death.' Jenny glanced over her shoulder to see Penny shrug.

'That's not my department. That will be up to the Coroner, Doc Holbrook, when we get her back to Adelaide. My job is to assess the body on scene, scour the possible crime scene or determine it's a secondary dump site and collect and collate any evidence on the body or on scene.'

'Wow. How long did you study for your job?' Jenny asked.

'The same eighteen months as a police cadet as you, but I'm a forensic scientist, so I needed a degree first. Four years of uni got me a forensic science degree, then once I finished at the academy, I specialised in Criminal Investigation to make sure I could bring the science and the procedure together.'

'How long you been on the job?'

'Four years fully qualified.'

'And they let you head up an investigation like this?'

'There aren't that many of us and the senior investigators don't often take rural scenes unless it's high profile. They are older, have families, and don't have to earn respect or prove themselves.'

'And they aren't women?'

'That too, but all up, science fortunately isn't quite as butch as the rest of the police force can be.'

'Hey, I'm right here you know,' Philips protested. 'We aren't all chauvinistic pricks.'

Neither woman answered and Philips watched Penny in his rear-view mirror as sunshine and instant heat began to fully embrace the day.

'Can I at least get some agreement on it?'

'Look Philips, you show me any man in this line of work that doesn't think he's tougher, more capable, even smarter or more suited to the work than a woman.'

The Constable was quiet a moment. 'Well I think you're definitely smarter than me.' Penny stifled a laugh, but Jenny wasn't giving up.

'But capable of defending myself against a big, nasty crim?'

'Don't mistake chivalry with chauvinism. They aren't the same. If you come up against a big, ugly crim, I tell you what, you can have first stab at him, but don't be surprised if I step in if he hurts you. That's just a guy thing.'

The girls smiled and Philips relaxed. 'Point taken.' Jenny offered a truce, her hands up in surrender. 'But I get first stab, right!' She waved her finger at him.

Philips took a deep breath and sighed. 'You got it.' He pulled the four-wheel-drive to a halt and got out, but Jenny waited for the dirt to drift past the vehicle before opening her door. The idea was absurd because she was going to be covered in red and white dust in no time.

She quelled her excitement. Having never been down a mine before was making her stomach flutter with anticipation. So far, Coober Pedy was certainly putting on a show. A dead body in a mine and her first ever visit to a Dugout—not that it was very impressive, but she was sure there were bigger, grander options to check out. At least she hoped so. Either way, it wasn't even twenty-four hours yet, and she was knee-deep in mystery.

Chapter 9

The temperature dropped dramatically as the women descended the steel ladder, bolted to the wall of the mine shaft. Jenny failed to notice it yesterday with all the rescue gear in the way.

'You don't suppose she came down here willingly?' she called down into the midnight black cavern below where the sound of Penny's boots on steel rung out with each footfall.

'I will know more once I examine the scene.' She reached the bottom and stepped from the ladder. Jenny did the same a few seconds later.

'Okay Philips, lower it down.' Penny called up through the opening where a cloudless blue sky hung, unaware of the death below. 'I feel like Santa Claus.' Penny's head-torch surveyed the mine walls with beams of light hitting the rough stone in all directions.

'I think that shaft is way bigger than a chimney, just between you and me.' Jenny resisted the urge to look at the forensic scientist, for fear her light beam would blind her.

They looked up as the winch started, the sound echoing down the shaft. A pallet of gear blocked the daylight from above. They strained and struggled as the equipment swung on the metal cable, finally managing to manoeuvre it away from the ladder into an open area that led to various tunnels and larger rooms.

Jenny stared at the walls illuminated by lamp light. The rock was solid, and once chipped or blasted away, the area appeared like a limestone cave with mottled white and orange sedimentary layers of stone. It reminded her of the tombs of Egypt, cut into sandstone bedrock. They needed no shoring up with boards or wooden beams.

'Amazing.' Jenny spun slowly around, taking in the scene.

Penny chuckled. 'Let's set these lights up. We have a body to put to rest and maybe a crime to solve.'

'Of course. Sorry. This whole experience is a little surreal.'

'Here, set this light up over there.' Penny pointed as Jenny wrestled with the cumbersome equipment.

'On it.'

Jenny wrangled the floodlight into position before opening and locking the tripod legs in place. Flicking the switch, she wriggled the light around so that it shone up toward the roof, throwing the space into near daylight.

They pulled on gloves, disposable covers on their shoes, and Penny wore a disposable suit over her clothing, which Jenny was quickly becoming jealous of.

'I'm on my way down,' Philips called from above.

'Okay,' Jenny called back before finally taking a moment to survey the scene in full light. This wasn't her first body recovery, but it was her first decomp and although the bones were down in the mine long enough for all muscle and tissue to dissolve, the faint smell of death still lingered.

The body was situated only a few metres away from where Pickard landed when he fell. With the surroundings now lit up, Jenny was reminded even more of her visit to the Egyptian tombs in the Valley of the Kings, except instead of paintings or hieroglyphics, these walls featured bore holes and chipped out channels—a road map to the cavern's history.

'Do you think they found opals here?' Jenny asked Philips as he reached the mine floor.

'Sure. This area is full of them. Not sure why they abandoned it though. Sometimes miners run out of money or some of these guys are loners and they die with no-one ever knowing they even held a claim out here.

'How long since this mine was abandoned?' Penny asked as she opened her forensic kit and pulled out a brush before putting her camera around her neck.

'You look like an archaeologist,' Jenny teased.

'I feel like one down in this pit. It's not often I work on bones. We'll need a forensic anthropologist to confer on this case.'

'I'll need to check who owns the claim and find out if anyone in town knows anything about when it was last used.'

'You can probably do that now if you want Philips. We'll be a while here and I'd rather not have too many feet stomping around while I work. The rescue team will have made enough mess already.'

'Oh. You okay down here on your own?' Philips squirmed, bit his lip and squirmed some more.

'The big, mean crims can't exactly sneak up on us now can they?' Jenny collected a sieve from the pallet of gear and began working out a grid pattern to commence her search for evidence.

'That's not what I meant, but okay, I'll head to town and find out who owns the claim. Do a little background check.'

'Thanks.' Penny was already distracted by the body in front of her. 'Send the ambulance out in an hour. I'll have her bagged up by then.'

'Will do.' Philips began the climb to the top.

Penny started taking photos of the body, using her brush to flick dirt away as she worked. 'You know Philips didn't mean anything sexist?'

Jenny peered up from her first tray of dirt, taking a moment to register what Penny was talking about.

'You think I'm being defensive?'

'Yep, just a little.' Penny snapped another two photos.

'You're probably right. The joys of working in a male dominated industry.'

'I hear you, but most of the guys I've met along the way aren't sure what to do with us girls on the job.' Penny took a close-up photo of some torn fabric. 'It's not like they mean to treat us differently, but we are different, whether we like it or not. This women's lib is all great, but guys are stuck in no man's land these days. Treat you like a little sister and they are deemed patronising. Treat you like an equal and they get in trouble for workplace harassment.'

'What do you mean?' Jenny struggled to hide her curiosity. She tried to focus on the job at hand, but Penny's comment confused her. 'I grew up dairy farming where everyone pulled their weight, male or female.'

'Exactly. So you see Philips' comment as patronising, but what if he really was your brother? Would you have taken it that way?'

Jenny thought a moment. *Would she?*

'Hey, check this out.' Penny was bagging loose pieces of the dead woman's clothing.

Jenny inched closer, being careful not to disturb anything. 'What's up?'

'Her knickers are gone and these tears aren't from the fall, at least I don't believe they are.'

'Rape?'

'The chances of proving that with nothing but bones to work with is very slim, but on face value, I think we are talking some type of sexual assault. A girl's underwear doesn't exactly go missing by mistake.'

'Maybe she didn't wear any?'

Penny screwed up her nose, then frowned, then shook her head as though she were confused. 'I guess that's possible. I'm ready to bag her now, give me a hand and we'll get her body on a plane to Adelaide. Maybe Doc can confirm her ID and then we can start asking the right questions of those who knew her well enough to answer the underwear question.'

Jenny snorted. 'Now that is going to be one very strange interview with her boyfriend and those closest to her.' The young constable pulled a face. 'Excuse me Sir, but can you recall if Tiffany made it a habit of getting around with no underwear?'

Penny laughed as she laid out a black plastic body bag and unzipped it. 'Better you than me. That's why I work with the dead.'

'For someone who works with the dead, you seem to know a lot about reading the living.'

Chapter 10

Jenny watched her uniforms roll around the front loading washing machine as the suds tried desperately to wash away the red dirt, now ingrained in the cotton material.

'Hey, I thought I might find you here.' Penny entered the laundry room, showered, changed and ready for dinner.

'I'm never going to see the real colour of these shoes again.' Jenny lifted her left leg—a red stained sandshoe dangled and she jiggled it for emphasis.

'That's the truth.'

'What's worse, is that these are the only shoes other than my work boots until my personal gear arrives.'

'I wish I could lend you a pair.' Jenny looked down at Penny's feet. They both laughed out loud. The forensic scientist was the same height as Jenny, only a far stockier build with feet at least two sizes larger.

'You going to be long? Tim and Nev are meeting us at the bar.' Penny grinned mischievously.

'I don't know Penny. I think I might call it an early night. I'm shagged.'

'You can't do that. It's my last night in town. I fly out in the morning.'

'Really. You're done already?'

'Body went to the Doc this morning. I've collected all the evidence I need on scene. The rest is up to you to get to the bottom of it.'

'Damn. I'm going to miss your moral support.'

'You'll be fine. Even more reason to get to know Tim and Nev better. The more locals you know, the easier life in this place will be.'

'As nice as the boys are, it's not the same. The girls here all look at me like I'm their worst enemy.'

'You're serious competition for them, that's all.'

'Competition. What on earth…?'

'For the guys. Have you totally missed the fact that Nev has been hovering since you got here?'

'I noticed, but he's just chasing another notch on his belt.'

'Exactly. Friends with benefits. Don't knock it.'

Jenny shook her head as the washing machine finished its final spin. 'Not interested.'

'In Nev?'

'In a fling.'

'Why?'

'I'm here for one reason and one reason only.'

'Your career.'

'No. To solve a family mystery.' Jenny pulled the washing out of the machine and placed it in the dryer before pressing the *On* button.

'What mystery?' Penny spoke quietly, looking over her shoulder like a schoolgirl sharing a smoke in the loos.

Jenny stopped, considering if telling Penny was wise. The forensic scientist was leaving tomorrow. The concept of having her in the city to run ideas past, as evidence came to light, could be advantageous.

'My aunt and cousin went missing after visiting Coober Pedy nine years ago. They were never found.

Penny whistled. 'So you took a job here to try and find out what happened?'

'Exactly.'

'Does the Sergeant know?'

'I don't think so. Williams is a common name.'

'I'd say he has an idea, or he will when you start digging.'

Jenny shrugged. 'I'll deal with that issue if it comes up.'

'Dinner then? We can run over this current case before I have to go back to Adelaide. Maybe you can tell me a little about your aunt and cousin too.'

'Let's not go there tonight, but I'll likely call on you for a favour if I get stuck.' Jenny's eyes drifted to the floor. 'If you don't mind?'

'Anytime.' Penny started for the door. 'Let's catch the boys.'

'Just a couple of beers, then I'm hitting the hay for an early night.'

'Just a couple.' Penny agreed with a twinkle in her eye that said *not on your life honey.*

****

'That's Cheryl Peterson.' Nev pointed to the snarky barmaid from the previous night and Jenny suddenly realised she'd not even bothered to put the woman's name in her databank, something a cop should always do – an indication she was still finding her feet in the hot, dry outback and unfamiliar town.

'No way! I should have picked that up when you spoke with her last night.'

'It's easy to not recall names when you first move to a new place.'

'I'm usually more on the ball.'

'So you think Tiffany is the dead body in the mine?'

'I shouldn't have told you. Keep it to yourself or I could be heading back to Adelaide faster than planned.'

'We wouldn't want that now.' Nev's expression was hard to read and Jenny decided she drunk one too many beers to bother trying.

'I'm heading to bed. We'll have another long day tracking down leads tomorrow.' *And I need to get my washing out of the dryer before I'm forced to iron it.* Jenny thought.

'One more.' Penny begged.

'What time are you leaving?'

'Seven thirty flight.'

'I'll see you before you go. But right now, I'm desperate for sleep.'

'I'll walk you to your room.' Nev got up, sculled the last mouthful of his beer and grabbed his car keys off the table in one smooth movement.

'I can find the way. I have to collect some laundry anyway.'

'I'm sure you can, but I'm good with a laundry detour. I should be heading off anyway. I'm on early shift tomorrow.' He wasn't taking no for an answer and Jenny couldn't muster enough energy to argue.

They left the bar, travelling past reception toward the laundry/ Jenny stopped. 'What's the history between you and Cheryl anyway?'

Nev's eyebrows rose. 'That obvious.' He bit his lip. His eyes left hers.

'I'm a cop. Reading people is what I do.' She turned and carried on, reaching the laundry around the corner and thankfully finding it still unlocked.

'Cheryl and I had a little fling, but that's Cheryl.'

'What does that mean?' Jenny pulled her uniform from the dryer and left the laundry room, heading towards her motel room.

'She's a nice chick, but she's,' he pursed his lips, looking for the right word, 'she's not girlfriend material.'

Jenny was getting frustrated with him beating around the bush. 'You mean she was just a one-night stand?'

'No. A four or five-night stand. This place is a little lonely at times.'

'And you're not looking for commitment.' Jenny took the key out of her pocket as she approached her door.

'I wouldn't say that, just Cheryl isn't my type.'

Jenny put her key in the lock, stopped turning to face Nev who was leaning against the doorframe, his arm above her head, the other touching the small of her back, caging her in.

'You are.'

Jenny laughed and pushed the door open. 'I bet that's what you told Cheryl. Good night Nev. Thanks for the company. I'll likely see you tomorrow.'

She rushed into her room, turning to close the door. For a split second, she thought Nev might shove his foot forward to stop her, but he didn't. Closing the door, she leant against it, hugging her laundry to her chest. Why was her heart racing?

Chapter 11

'The pathologist in Adelaide has confirmed our dead body is Tiffany Cox. Dental records are a match.' O'Connell sat on the corner of the desk. 'At this stage, we could be looking at an accident or something else. For now, it's just an unexplained death, but we need to cover all bases so that once the Coroner makes a ruling, we are ready to either put this case to bed or move forward.'

Philips handed Jenny a coffee and she resisted the urge to smell it. So far, she was yet to find a decent brew in Coober Pedy. Beer aplenty, but the coffee was all instant, watery crap or drip filtered and stewed on a hotplate for hours.

Making the effort to be polite, she took a small sip and tried to keep her face passive. It was a far cry from the cappuccinos she was used to and the thought made her homesick for the little seaside cafes and lush green parklands of Victor Harbor. But in the big scheme of things, it was only coffee. A poor woman was dead and she was charged with the job of discovering how and why.

'She had no knickers on Sir, so I'm calling foul play.' Jenny put her hand up like she was in school calling dibs.

'And your years of experience make your judgement so valid Williams.' O'Connell's curled lip softened his words as Jenny resisted the urge to roll her eyes skyward.

Instead, she ignored the comment like a dutiful junior constable. Maybe O'Connell was right. Maybe she was being arrogant and jumping to conclusions. 'Mark said Cheryl was her friend. We can start there? Find out when she last saw her friend?'

'You do that Williams. Philips.' The constable put his coffee down, eager to move on his orders. 'Find out what's taking Mines and Energy so friggin' long. We need to know who owns that mine and why no one discovered Tiffany's body earlier.'

'Will do.'

'Did the pathologist have a time of death yet Sir?' Jenny took another polite sip of her coffee, then put it down at the back of the service desk, vowing to dispose of it discreetly later.

'No, they need an anthropologist to age the bones. That, together with information on her last known sighting should give us a timeline.'

'I'll head to the motel now.' Jenny went to her locker and stopped. A photo of her, Penny and Nev, looking dishevelled was stuck to the door. She pulled it off and turned, shaking it in her hand. 'Very funny guys.'

Philips laughed loudly, giving himself away, but O'Connell's lip turned up, not ruling him out as an accomplice. Jenny continued to get her utility vest out, check her service weapon and carry on like nothing had happened.

Philips lifted the phone and made a call to chase down the mine ownership details again as Jenny left the station, throwing the photo in the waste paper bin on the way past O'Connell's desk.

At least she wasn't digging in the dirt again today. Penny was happy they'd searched the immediate area around the body thoroughly. The scene was still taped off, in case they needed to take another look but for now, she was back to natural ground level.

'Jenny. You look a little more spry this morning.' Marj grinned.

'Well I managed to get out before the karaoke started again last night didn't I?'

'Oh, come on now. You put on a great show. The locals are still talking about it.'

'That's what I was afraid of.'

'What can I do for you?'

'Here on business Marj. What time does Cheryl's shift start?'

'Why? Is this about that body in the mine? I heard it was Tiffany, cut up into little pieces.'

Jenny laughed, but a tingle at the back of her neck made her wonder how Marj knew it was Tiffany already?

'I can confirm the body was that of Tiffany Cox, but to the rest, that's just cocky poop Marj. Where on earth did you hear that?' The older woman grinned and Jenny realised she was just hunting for clues.

'Tiffany and Cheryl go back a ways. Cheryl moved here with her boyfriend to mine. That didn't go so well. He offed himself and she didn't have claim to his mine, so she started working at the pub here. She was just eighteen back then.'

'Who was her boyfriend?' Jenny used her mobile phone to take notes. Something not encouraged by the academy, but she wasn't a pencil and paper girl.

'Jacob Henderson. He was a lot older than her, about thirty-five I think. Drinker, smoker, druggy. Never did manage to make much of the mining. Too lazy.'

'And how did Cheryl and Tiffany get to know each other?'

'Kindred spirits I guess. Both had excessively nasty upbringings from all accounts. No family to speak of, or at least none that either ever mentioned. It's a bit of a love triangle, although I'm not sure love had anything to do with it. Tiffany and Cheryl lived with Jacob before he died.

'What happened to Tiffany after Jacob died?'

'They were…how can I put this. They had to make ends meet. Let's put it that way. Tiffany had a few clients, until Mark Nesbitt convinced her he'd look after her.'

Jenny's cheeks flushed. 'Working girls.'

Marj laughed. 'Let's just say they didn't pay room and board. I'm not sure you can call it work if you don't actually get paid, but it certainly wasn't pleasure either.'

'Thanks Marj. What time can I catch up with Cheryl?'

The red-headed manager turned to the clock on the wall. 'You'll find her in the dining room having an early lunch now before her shift starts.'

'Thanks.' Jenny turned to leave.

'So how did Tiffany die then?' The cheer was gone from her face and Jenny could see unshed tears in the woman's eyes.

'It's too early to tell.'

'I hope it was just a fall.'

'Me too.' Jenny was almost certain it wasn't but she kept the thought to herself. For now.

****

'I last saw her at the Opal Festival in June.' Cheryl used a paper napkin to blow her nose and wipe the tears from her cheeks.

'Did she say anything about leaving town?'

'No. Not to me.'

'What about having a rich boyfriend?'

'Tiffany always dreamed about a rich boyfriend.'

'But she didn't say she'd found one?'

'No.'

Something was niggling at Jenny's subconscious. 'Did Tiffany ever date anyone other than Mark?'

'Date.' Cheryl managed a stifled laugh.

'See?' Jenny pushed.

'Look. I'm sure if you haven't found out already, you soon will. Tiffany probably slept with just about every guy in town who could buy her a drink or pay for dinner. Doctor Neville Newman included.'

Jenny wasn't sure why Nev was being singled out. 'Is the Doctor particularly relevant?'

Cheryl shrugged and for a second Jenny wondered if she was being evasive on purpose.

'Just thought you should know.'

'Noted.' Now she was beginning to understand the random reference to Nev. 'Do you know anyone who would do her any harm?'

'No.'

'Any reason she would have been out at night wandering around the mine shafts.'

'Noodling maybe?' Cheryl shrugged one shoulder. 'But that wasn't Tiffany's thing. She left Mark because she hated the dark. Even the upper floor of Mark's place made her uncomfortable. Claustrophobic.'

'Coober Pedy is probably the worst place for a claustrophobic.'

'I agree, but she had no other place to go.' Cheryl's eyes held a sadness Jenny was unfamiliar with. These girls had experienced more hardship, more pain than most people endured in a lifetime.

'Thanks Cheryl. I have no idea what you're going through, but I know it must be hard reliving this.' In reality, she knew exactly how it felt. At least Cheryl hadn't known Tiffany was lost and now she'd been found dead, Cheryl would have closure. But Jenny didn't have any of that. That's what she was in Coober Pedy for… 'I'll let you know if I need anything else, but if you think of anything, anything at all, no matter how small, please let me know.'

'I will.' Cheryl wiped her nose again before forcing herself to eat a mouthful of coleslaw—her appetite obviously now gone.

She left Cheryl in the restaurant, wondering why Tim and Nev hadn't mentioned Tiffany's bedroom services to her last night, when the girl's name had come up. Maybe they didn't know, but Cheryl said Nev did know and even if Cheryl was making that up, she found it hard to believe in such a small, tight knit community that they hadn't heard.

She needed to go to the bathroom, so decided to call in to her own room for a quick freshen up. The heat of the day was building and all she wanted to do right now was strip off and go to the pool for a swim before heading back to the station, but she would have to settle for a cool splash of water from the basin in her bathroom.

She entered the darkened room and with the blinds drawn she could savour the coolness a moment. Putting her keys on the dresser, she noticed the postcard from Melanie and studied it closely a moment. The main picture featured the town sign, but the two side photos showed the William Creek station and pub. They'd thought it a hoot that the pub and station held their namesake and Jenny knew they'd planned to make a visit.

That would be one of the first places she'd begin her search. Maybe someone would remember them? Chances were slim, but she knew they'd booked a trip to experience a farm stay in the bush, including a two-day horseback trail ride across William Creek Station. She never found out if the police asked about that part of the trip.

She was only seventeen—no one interviewed her about Melanie's disappearance. Maybe her uncle didn't know she'd received the postcard? Surely he did. She expected to sneak access to the file soon.

Since moving to Coober Pedy, it wouldn't be unusual to chase up an old case. She'd never dared try from Victor Harbor, it might have been flagged. The computer systems were getting more advanced all the time and there'd be no excuse to access a missing persons file from over nine years ago in a different region.

A quick trip to the bathroom, a cool wash, a reapplication of SPF 15 foundation and she was set to head out into the heat once more.

Tiffany! She had to focus on what had happened to Tiffany for now. Getting side tracked wasn't an option. Was the girl killed by a stalker, an upset client, an ex-lover?

Who was the rich guy Mark spoke about or was he a work of fiction? Something to get them off Mark's case? That could make sense, since Tiffany never told Cheryl she was moving away or had a new boyfriend.

She crossed the road to the station to find O'Connell and Philips deep in conversation.

'What's up?'

'Just found out who the claim belongs to.' Philips looked like the cat who had eaten the canary.

'And?'

'Jacob Henderson. He…'

'Killed himself.' Jenny finished and Philips frowned.

'How'd you know?' He seemed disappointed, as though he'd hoped to impress her with his local knowledge.

'I was just talking with Marj, at the motel. She said Tiffany and Cheryl *both* used to live with him before he killed himself.'

'Yep, he was a weird guy.' Philips turned to O'Connell for confirmation. The Senior Constable only nodded.

'You didn't tell me Tiffany *and* Cheryl were local…' Jenny left the last word unsaid.

'Tramps,' O'Connell offered.

'Not politically correct.' Jenny tried to keep the tone neutral. 'Let's try escorts.'

'That's a little too classy,' Philips suggested. 'I didn't think of it to be honest. Neither Cheryl nor Tiffany have been on the job for a few years and they only did it to make ends meet. There aren't many female miners out here and there are only so many bar jobs and check out chicks wanted around town.'

'Surely the tourism sector employ plenty of female workers?'

'Some, but tourism is seasonal and the age-old profession has always followed miners around.' O'Connell started typing on the keyboard once more.

'It doesn't sound like Tiffany exactly had a roaring trade or money rolling in with it.'

'Tiffany wasn't a professional. She kind of went from guy to guy, trying to find a good one. I thought she'd settled down with Mark.'

Mark hardly seemed like a 'good one', but Jenny let the comment slide anyway. 'So, you don't believe Mark is capable of killing her or find it strange or a weird coincidence she ended up dead in her pimp's mine?'

'Slow down a second. We don't know she *was* murdered yet and what makes you say Jacob was her pimp?'

'Older guy, takes two, what eighteen-year-olds under his roof and feeds them from the goodness of his heart, and for his own pleasure and nothing else?'

'I know a lot of guys who'd be happy with that.' Philips grinned at O'Connell. The Senior Constable shook his head, frowned, then returned his attention to Jenny with focussed eyes. She took it as permission to continue.

'But he was a drinker, a druggy. Are we sure he killed himself? Plus, I guarantee Tiffany's death comes back murder. Don't forget there was no underwear on the victim when she died.'

'Wait up there Williams. This is the bush. We don't have organised crime syndicates working here. If Jacob was pimping the girls out, he was doing it off his own bat.' O'Connell waved his hand at Jenny. 'And we just established she was a pro, no underwear isn't conclusive.'

'Are you sure you don't have organised crime here? I'm reasonably certain there's organised crime everywhere.'

Chapter 12

Jenny's phone pinged with a text. She retrieved her phone to read the message. *Sorry about last night. How about a dip in the pool? Nev.*

Her shirt was stuck to her back, her hair limp from the heat. She didn't need any encouragement. Her fingers typed quickly. *You bring the beer. What time?*

Six.

See u there.

Jenny glanced at her watch and checked over her shoulder. Philips had already left for the day. Sarge too. Only O'Connell remained, sitting at his desk, fingers tapping on the keyboard, eyes focussed on the screen.

Jenny sighed. Accessing his computer was going to be impossible. Instead, she decided the front counter computer would have to do. It was less private and anyone walking past could peer over her shoulder, but with everyone else gone, it was a risk she was going to have to take.

'You going to be much longer Williams?' O'Connell looked up as he turned his desk top monitor off.

'Only five minutes Sir. Just filing a final report on my interview with Cheryl.'

'You good to close up behind you then?'

'Sure.'

'Okay, just pull the door closed. It will lock automatically.'

'Will do.'

O'Connell left and Jenny sighed in relief. It was so less stressful being alone. Now she could search the database for the file she needed without fear of being exposed. She entered the details—*Williams, Melanie and Carolyn.* Clicking the send button, she waited, tapping her fingers on the mouse impatiently. The file number came up. She took a slow, steady breath before clicking it open.

All the usual details were included—names, ages, missing person report information as filed by her uncle. The investigating officer had made some inquiries in Coober Pedy, but nothing had come of them. An interview with the accommodation owner, a tour operator and a booking agency in town. Nothing mentioned about a tour to William Creek.

Jenny began to wonder if maybe they didn't go after all, but she was sure they were adamant they wanted to. The note on the postcard indicated they'd booked the trip, but if the local booking agency had no knowledge, who had they booked with? Directly maybe?

Jenny printed out the file, thankful that at least the station had a laser printer. Five minutes later she was flicking the lights off and pulling the front door closed.

Back in her room, she placed the file on the top shelf of her wardrobe, not wanting anyone to accidentally find it on display. Fortunately, she'd packed a swimsuit in her suitcase, which she changed into before throwing on the only dress she'd managed to bring with her. The very same one she'd worn the night before. Hopefully her gear arrived soon or she'd be spending more time in the laundry room.

Slinging her backpack over her shoulder, she locked the front door and headed for the local kebab shop. If Nev was bringing the beer, she'd bring the food.

Twenty minutes later they were sitting together, with a can of beer in one hand, a chicken kebab in the other.

'I think I need to get wet before I eat. I'm so hot.' Jenny put her food down on the bench and covered the kebab with her towel to keep the thousands of flies away while she took a quick swim.

'I'll watch.'

'Really?' Jenny's eyebrows rose as she slipped her dress off over her head.

Nev chuckled. 'Not that I won't enjoy the show, but I need this beer. I didn't get a lunch break because we had an accident on the highway—two adult males and one female all brought in. One passenger was in terrible shape.'

'Tell me about it in a sec. I really need this swim to cool off. I've been dreaming about it all day.'

Nev nodded and took a huge bite of his kebab. His eyes rolled back as a moan left his lips.

Diving into the water was like rolling in silk. She opened her eyes to see legs and feet treading water around her as the coolness slowly lowered her core temperature.

Two laps later she pulled herself up to the side and stood, making her way to her towel. The striped blue and white cotton fabric was thin and had seen better days, but it was all that was in her room.

Wrapping it around her body, she tossed her dress out of the way to keep it dry and retrieved the kebab, opening the foil wrapping. The aroma hit her senses, making her stomach grumble. Nev chuckled.

'What, I missed lunch too, but this heat is a shocker. If I didn't cool down first I'd likely just throw it all back up at you.' She took a bite of her kebab to stop another wave of stomach grumbles.

'You'll get used to it. Everyone finds it hard at first.'

'Did they all make it?' Jenny asked before taking another big bite, garlic aioli running down her fingers and dripping to the pavement.

'Yep, although the girl—she was in the back without a seat belt by the looks. She's not critical, but her face was all cut up so they airlifted her to Adelaide for plastic surgery after we stabilized her.'

'How long have you lived here?' She took a sip of beer before another bite of kebab.

'Five years. Came up shortly after finishing my internship.'

'You didn't tell me you knew Tiffany well.'

Nev choked on his mouthful, before holding his finger up to indicate he needed to stop choking before he could answer the question.

'Well! That's not exactly true.' Nev gawked at Jenny. She studied him a moment. How far could she push their new friendship? On one hand, she didn't want to create a wall between them, but on the other, she had a case to solve and Nev hadn't exactly been totally on the up and up with her.

'You didn't fill me in on her….occupation.'

Nev laughed. 'Tiffany was a lost soul, who threw herself into the arms of just about anyone who opened them.'

'And you opened them.' It wasn't a question and Nev rubbed his chin before answering.

'I see where this is going. You have me pegged already. Measured and weighed wanting.'

'Not at all. What you do with your personal life is up to you. I just wondered why you didn't mention you had a history with Tiffany. Since she's dead now.'

'Hang on a minute. Are you asking me on a personal level? Like you want to know how many women I've slept with before you hang out with me? Or are you asking on a professional level? If it's the latter, I don't particularly like the idea one little bit. I invited you out to apologise.'

'Yeah about that.'

'Look, I was a jerk last night. You're not…'

'Tiffany or Cheryl?'

'Right.'

'No I'm not, but they deserve or deserved more respect than they got.'

There was a moment of silence as Jenny took another mouthful of food, chewed aggressively and watched as Nev's face changed expression a multitude of times.

'Look. I get it. You're a guy. Sometimes you're ruled by basic instinct but sometimes you need to be accountable for that too.'

'What are you saying?'

'I'm saying, Tiffany is dead and the guys in this town had the chance to help her, keep her safe, but they didn't.'

Nev studied his beer, then ripped away another piece of his food, chewing it like it had suddenly turned into cardboard. He swallowed. Hard. 'You're right. I'm not proud of myself. Medical school is kind of loose. Then intern years are even crazier with long shifts, hard work and hard play.'

'I like you Nev but I'm focussed on my career.' She was focussed on other things like what happened to her aunt and cousin, but she wasn't ready to share any of that yet.

'I am too.'

'Yes, but you're looking for something I can't offer you. I know this is the speech that every guy hates to hear, but it's the truth, from the bottom of my heart, we are friends Nev and I don't do friends with benefits.'

Nev took yet another bite of his cardboard kebab followed by another long, slow sip of beer to wash it down.

'I can live with that.'

'Are you sure?'

'Intelligent conversation isn't easy to find around here and your friendship is worth a lot to me.'

Jenny smiled. 'I'm glad you said that. I'd hate to alienate my first friend in town.'

Nev finished his beer, screwed up his rubbish and got up to put it in the bin. Returning to his seat, he plonked down, took a measured breath and reset his expression before speaking. 'Any updates on Tiffany's death?'

Jenny frowned with a mouth full, then swallowed hard. 'I shouldn't discuss the case.' She'd said too much the night before and as an ex-client come lover, Nev shouldn't be in on any developments until they discovered if Tiffany was murdered or her death was accidental.

'Tell me about the accident.'

'A roll over on the Sturt Highway.'

'Locals?'

'From neighbouring stations, yeah. One from the William Creek Station, the other works at Downing Station next door, and one is the William Creek publican's son.'

'Shit.' Jenny thought about the accident. The police would have to make a report and she was suddenly desperate to be assigned that duty. 'Are they all going to be okay?'

'The girl, like I said had to be airlifted to Adelaide, but the other two are recovering. The driver had only superficial injuries, the male passenger scored a broken collarbone from the seatbelt, but it saved his life from all accounts. The S.E.S. said the car was crushed, totally written off.'

'I guess I'll be making a few inquiries about that one tomorrow then?'

'Probably, although the highway patrol accident investigation team will have already finished up on the accident scene. I'm not sure how the jurisdiction works.'

'Usually, they will hand their findings over to the local police to follow up. Was alcohol involved?'

'No. Sounds like an argument broke out and the driver got distracted. Drove the four-wheel drive off the road and rolled it into the drainage ditch.'

Jenny got up, put her own rubbish in the bin before hanging her towel over the seat to dry. 'Ready for that swim now?'

'For sure.'

Chapter 13

'Williams!' Jenny barely set foot in the station before Sarge screamed out her name. The hairs on the back of her neck rose at the tone.

'Sir?' She strode into his office at the rear of the small building, her bag still over her shoulder.

'You need to interview two clowns at the hospital. They were involved in an accident yesterday.'

'Heard about that from Nev Sir. Have the crash investigation team finished with the report?'

'That's not your concern. I just want statements from the two bozos that were arguing. They nearly got the poor girl in the back of the car killed. She'll be disfigured for life.'

'We don't know the circumstances until I get those statements Sir?'

The sergeant's face grew red, his eyes said he was ready to knock someone's block off. Jenny wondered what had him so worked up, but wisely said nothing.

'Just go to the hospital and do the interviews Williams.'

'Yes Sir.' She saluted, turned and left the sergeant's office. As she passed O'Connell, he gave her a sympathetic look.

'Any word on Tiffany's case?' Jenny asked O'Connell as she stopped in front of the bank of lockers that occupied most of the side wall of the main office area. She put her backpack in one, before retrieving her utility vest complete with Taser. Turning to O'Connell, she caught the keys to the weapons safe, thrown before she even asked for them.

'Not yet. I'll chase the forensic team in Adelaide later. They don't start work as early as us.'

Jenny took out her service weapon, checked the safety was on and then locked the cabinet before returning the keys to the Senior Constable.

'What was that all about?' she whispered, her eyebrows indicating Sarge's office, but O'Connell shook his head. He wasn't answering her question, at least not within earshot of the Sergeant.

'I'll interview the guys at the hospital. Nev said they are from the William Creek area. Do we need to head out and find out more?' She hoped the answer would be yes, but unless there was something suspicious about the cause of the crash, then her excuse to get out there was probably not going to be this crash after all.

'See what the statements turn up.'

'Will do. Where is Philips?' Jenny turned around to survey the office.

'He's following up on a domestic.'

'Oh. That sucks. Which car can I take to the hospital then?'

'Grab mine. You can team up with Philips when he gets back.'

'Thanks.' She caught the keys O'Connell tossed her.

Fifteen minutes later she entered the hospital reception area. The low set building appeared to have been constructed in the seventies, with modular panels like the old primary school buildings she remembered from her school days.

'I'm Constable Williams, here to see the two male patients from the accident yesterday.' A male nurse in his late thirties didn't have to refer to any lists or computers to know who she was looking for.

'Down the hall, third door on your right. Room 3, B and C beds.' He seemed disinterested but Jenny quickly realised he was simply busy, as the phone rang and there was no one else to answer it but him. He sighed and picked up the receiver.

She waved a thank you and wandered down the hall, jumping aside to narrowly miss bumping into Nev as he came out of the ward.

'Hey. Morning,' he grinned. 'You here to interview these two?' She nodded and Nev stepped aside, then guided her into the ward.

'Sam, Mick. This is Constable Williams. She'll have a few questions before you leave.' One patient was pulling on leather riding boots that covered the bottom of his faded denim jeans. The other was struggling with a sling, trying to get his shirt to sit over his shoulder, the sleeve hanging loosely.

'You two off already?' She glanced at Nev for confirmation.

'Yeah, they stayed in last night for observation, in case of concussion, but other than Mick's broken collarbone, they are all good.'

'Well I need to ask you some questions before you head back to William Creek. Is that okay with you?' Not that either of them had a choice and they knew it.

Both men grunted in the affirmative, avoiding eye contact with her and each other.

'Usually I'd do this one at a time, but since you are already in the same room, you have probably discussed the accident at length.'

The men shrugged. Sam was tall, broad shouldered and narrow in the hips. He wore his cowboy boots like he owned the world, his chest shoved out, his face set in a *don't mess with me* kind of expression.

Mick was shorter, stockier and wore a beard that was a cross between Ned Kelly bushranger and ZZ Top bikie style.

'Why don't you sit over here?' Jenny waved Sam over to Mick's bed as she pulled up a chair next to them.

'I'll catch you after work.' Nev gave Jenny a wave and left the ward. She watched him leave before returning her attention to the two young men.

'I'm going to record this.' They nodded in unison as Jenny put her phone on *record* and Sam sat down next to Mick. 'Who was driving?' She was certain it wasn't Mick. Nev had already said the passenger had broken his collarbone and the driver was unscathed.

'I was.' She turned her attention to Sam who almost put his hand up like a school kid, his confidence waning. She wondered if she made him think of an older sister or a teacher.

He was likely only eighteen, maybe nineteen years old and Jenny wondered how twenty-five had suddenly become old to anyone. Then she recalled how she'd gone to her friend's older brother's birthday party at the age of sixteen and couldn't imagine turning a quarter of a century. It just seemed so far away back then.

'Okay, Sam. I'll need your full name first.'

'Samuel William Johnston.'

'Age?'

'Nineteen.'

She went through the formalities before launching into the report of the accident.

'Okay guys. I'm still waiting on the accident report from the crash team, so why don't you tell me what happened?'

'I was driving back to William Creek after we came into town to pick up a few things.' Jenny turned to Mick. He nodded.

'Then what happened?'

'We were talking, about Tiffany.'

'Tiffany?' Jenny's ears pricked up, but she kept her face neutral. 'Do you know her?'

'We did. We found out she'd been found…'

'Dead.' Mick offered when Sam didn't seem able to say the word.

'You knew her well then?' Jenny's eyes penetrated Sam's but he broke eye contact and stared at his hands that fidgeted in his lap.

'She used to work at my dad's pub.' Mick offered his friend a reprieve from Jenny's questioning stare.

'William Creek pub?'

'Yeah, but a few years back.' Jenny locked the information away for later and focussed on the accident report.

'Okay, back to the accident. You were talking about Tiffany and then what?'

'We started arguing.'

'What about? Tiffany?'

'Sort of, not really.' Mick was doing all the talking. Sam kept his eyes on his hands that continued fidgeting in his lap.

'Charlie was angry.'

'Charlie? Who is Charlie?'

'The other person with us.' Mick again.

'The girl who had to be airlifted to Adelaide?'

Sam sighed, as though the weight of the world had landed on his shoulders. 'Yeah, she's kind of my girlfriend.'

'Kind of?'

'We hook up sometimes.'

'So it's casual?'

'Well I thought it was. But when she found out about Tiffany, she went right off. That's what we were arguing about.'

'So you got distracted, and crashed.'

'Not exactly.' Mick jumped in as if he needed to save his friend. 'Charlie punched him in the back of the head.'

Jenny fought to keep the shock from her face. 'So it wasn't casual after all?'

'It seems not.' Sam rubbed the back of his head partly as a self-conscious act, but then he rubbed it as though it still hurt.

'Did she knock you out?'

'No, but I was dazed a second. That's when I veered to the left.'

'I reached out to try and pull the wheel back, get us back on the road, but I pulled too hard.' Mick demonstrated as he spoke. 'The car changed direction too quickly and the wheels locked up on the loose dirt at the verge. We were all flung around like ragdolls, then we went down the ditch and the car rolled over.' His face went pale. 'We must have flipped twice, maybe more.'

'Okay boys. I'll type up these statements. I'll need email addresses so I can send you a digital copy. If anything doesn't sound right, you let me know. Okay?'

Jenny got up from the chair to leave but stopped as Sam spoke quietly. 'Am I going to be charged?'

'I'll hand this over and we'll need to get Charlie's statement, but if what you say is true, I don't think so, but it isn't up to me. It's up to my Sergeant. Do you know Sergeant Mackenzie?'

They nodded, their eyes suddenly a little wide.

'I'm new here, so you likely know better than me if he'll bring charges.'

'He probably will.' Sam sighed.

'Why do you say that?' Jenny put her phone in the leather pouch on her utility vest.

The boys exchanged a glance, Mick nodded.

'His daughter was killed in a car crash, out on Painted Desert Road about ten years back. He has a pretty short fuse when it comes to hooning in cars now.'

'Oh. That's horrible. I didn't know. But you weren't hooning, were you?'

'No way. We were just heading home.'

'Well if all the statements check out, you should be all good then.' Jenny now appreciated why the sergeant was so upset about the accident. 'I'll see if I can put in a good word for you.'

The young men smiled sheepishly. 'If your story checks out mind you.' They nodded they understood. 'You said Charlie was annoyed when you talked about Tiffany. Did you have a relationship with her Sam?'

'No, not a relationship, we just hooked up, but almost everyone in town hooked up with Tiffany at one time or another.'

Jenny nodded as her thoughts drifted to poor Tiffany. She'd not had the best life. Hopefully she hadn't met a nasty end. With any luck, she'd just died in a fall, because if she'd been murdered—Jenny shuddered at the long list of suspects they'd be dealing with.

'Someone picking you up?' Jenny strolled toward the exit, looking over her shoulder as she waited for their answer. She came to an abrupt halt, her chest slamming into a wall of chequered shirt and muscle.

'Yeah. I am.'

At nearly six-feet tall, she had to step back to see a dark blonde guy in his late twenties. His rough jawline revealed he hadn't stopped to shave this morning. The scent of his cologne said the look was intentional.

Distracted, Jenny forced herself to focus. 'Sorry about that. I'm Constable Williams. You are?' The man looked her up and down, but didn't respond.

'Sam, Mick. Let's go. I've got a ton of work to get back to.'

'Pleased to meet you too.' Jenny didn't bother to hold back the sarcasm.

'You finished with them I assume? You *were* heading out, weren't you?' He returned her tone with extra hot sauce.

'This is my brother. Nick.' Sam offered as he scooted past her, Mick following close behind.

'Let's go. Now already.' Nick didn't stop. He turned behind the two younger men and left without a backward glance.

Chapter 14

Jenny returned to the station, still puzzled over Nick Johnston's sour persona. 'Thanks for the loan.' She gently tossed the keys to O'Connell's car onto his desk. 'Just met Nick Johnston.'

'How did that go?'

'He's a sour puss, isn't he?'

'He's a good guy at heart. Just taken on a lot.'

'Really?' Jenny wanted to ask more, but why? Was it pertinent to Tiffany's case, or even her missing relatives? Unlikely. Why Nick Johnston was a rude arse was certainly not something she had time to concentrate on.

'Did you get anything out of the boys?'

'Yes, actually it was informative. They were arguing with Charlie who was sitting in the back seat. She distracted Sam with a punch to the back of his head. Both boys said the same thing, but obviously we'll need to interview Charlie to confirm.'

'That will hopefully settle the boss down a little. All morning, he's been like a dingo caught in a trap.'

'That bad.' Jenny showed O'Connell her most sympathetic face. 'Another thing the boys mentioned was that they were arguing about Tiffany.'

'Why?' O'Connell frowned, forcing his thick eyebrows together.

'They'd heard about her death and Tiffany used to work out at William Creek Pub, Mick's parents place. Did you know that?'

'No, can't say I did. It's not exactly my Local though.'

Jenny had no idea exactly how far away William Creek was, but everything was a long way between stops out in the bush. 'I think it could be worth a look. Question her old employers. Maybe they know something?'

'If she died of a fall, we'll not bother with that Williams. The Creek is over two hours away and the road is rough as guts.'

'Do we know any more about cause of death?'

'Bring up the case and let's have a look. I've not received any calls about it.' Jenny realised that she was more eager than anyone else in the station to find out how and why Tiffany had died.

Moving to the counter computer, she typed in a few details. The case number appeared on screen with attachments, yet to be opened. She scanned them for the autopsy report. Nothing. 'I'll call Penny in the forensic lab. Maybe she can speed it up.'

'You go for it girl. Good luck speeding up anything from the city crew. I'm sure they believe we have nothing better to do than wait around for them to grace us with info.'

Jenny grinned. 'Where's Philips?' She picked up the office phone and dialled the Forensic Lab number.

'He's picking up a friend from the airport.'

'Who's that?' The phone dial tone began to ring.

'You'll meet him soon enough I'm sure.'

'Forensics.' Jenny recognised her new friend's voice.

'Penny. Just the person I wanted to talk to.'

'Jen. How's it going? Settling in okay?'

'Sure, met a few locals. Went to the pool last night, it was great.'

'With anyone I know?'

Jenny laughed. 'Just a friend. How's our case going? Anything to report that hasn't made it into the file yet?'

'You in a hurry on this for any reason? Things a bit quiet out in the sticks?' Jenny could hear the laughter in Penny's voice.

'Busy enough, but I've got a hunch we are dealing with a murder. Either way I'd like to put this case to bed.'

'Let me check for you. It's been pretty hectic here since I got back.'

'Anything interesting?'

'It's always interesting.' Penny was silent, just the sound of keys clicking on a keyboard as she rummaged through the files. 'Here it is. Okay, I can see Doc's file on our system, but it's not been uploaded to the case file yet. Cause of death….hmm.'

'Penny!'

'Yeah, okay. Your gut is on point. The Doc found the victim's hyoid bone fractured.'

'Strangled?'

'It looks like it. I've been running an analysis from the victim's hair found on the body. It hasn't finished yet, but I will put a rush on it now and see if we can pull a tox screen from it. I'll upload it as soon as I get it.'

'Thanks Penny. I appreciate you putting a rush on it.'

'No problem. The least I can do for my karaoke wing man.'

Jenny laughed. 'See ya.'

'Bye.' Hanging up, she turned to update O'Connell as Philips entered with a short, broad guy that made her think of a dwarf from Lord of the Rings.

O'Connell got up to greet the newcomer. 'Len, good to see you mate. How's Perth treating you?'

'A lot cooler than here, that's for sure.' The man was heavily muscled with a broad forehead that made him look like a prize fighter who'd done too many rounds over the years.

'Len, this is our new constable. Williams, meet your predecessor, Len Holmes.'

Jenny watched the newcomer's face change from studying her, to a smile. 'Pleased to meet you Williams.'

'Jenny, you can call me Jenny since you're not on the job here, at least I'm guessing you're not?' She turned to Philips for confirmation.

'Len's just here to catch up with a few mates. Couldn't stay away from the place hey Len?'

Len didn't look at Philips, his eyes were fixed on Jenny, studying her like she was a puzzle he hadn't yet solved.

'I've got to follow up on a few leads. Philips, can you give me a lift out to William Creek Pub?' She glanced at Philips, who diverted his gaze to O'Connell.

'It's homicide then?' O'Connell asked and Jenny nodded. 'Okay Williams, follow the lead and let me know how you go. I'll cover the fort here today.'

'But Sir, it's a four-hour round trip without interviewing anyone.' Philips pouted. 'Len's come up for a visit and I'll miss the drinks tonight.'

'I can probably find my own way, if I can use your car.' Jenny held out her hand for the keys.

'Does the Sat-Nav work in your vehicle out there Philips? We don't want to lose our new constable on her first week in town.'

'Sure does. You just need to wiggle the extension aerial if it doesn't.'

'Okay. I'll find my way there.'

'What's the murder case? Don't get too many of them out here.' Len's question seemed casual.

'It's a local case Len. No need to worry about it.' She sounded defensive, even to her own ears. Maybe coming face

82

to face with her predecessor was more intimidating than she wanted, but she didn't think Len needed any details.

'Tiffany's body was found a few days ago.' Jenny resisted the urge to roll her eyes.

'Yeah, heard about that. Sad. Thought she'd left town.'

'That's what Mark thought too.' Philips lifted the counter. 'I'll bring him in for questioning then Sir?'

Len's eyebrows rose as he put two and two together. 'You think Tiffany was murdered?'

'Seems so. That's the homicide Williams was just talking about. She just got off the phone with Adelaide's forensic lab,' O'Connell answered, watching Philips and Len as he spoke. Jenny sighed. Well it seemed O'Connell wasn't as concerned about keeping the murder under wraps as she was.

'Shit. That's nasty.' Len replied after a short silence. 'Any leads?'

'You leave it to us Len. You're here on holidays mate. Catch up with your friends while your wife's not around to spoil your fun. Leave the cop work to us, hey.' O'Connell returned to his desk. 'Philips, drop Len off at the motel and then go get Mark.'

'Will do Sir. Come on Len, let's get you sorted.' Jenny started out with the two men. She opened the driver's side door of Philips' Landcruiser as Len took his duffle bag from the rear cargo area.

'I might miss drinks tonight Len, so enjoy yourself. Philips, see you tomorrow.'

'See ya.' He waved and turned with Len to head over the road to the motel.

Chapter 15

Jenny stopped the car and got out. After giving the antenna a tweak, she got back in and checked her location on the in-car navigation system. She was heading in the right direction, but she should have been at William Creek by now.

All she'd seen was miles of red dirt and the occasional outcrop of saltbush. She started the car and continued driving toward outbuildings visible in the distance.

As she drew closer, she could see a worn low-set building that resembled a shed. The front of the pub featured signage with XXXX Gold beer logos and the words *William Creek Hotel, Gateway to the Simpson Desert.* The sign said there was accommodation, but as Jenny got out and looked around, all she could see was an outbuilding, a windsock and a light aircraft parked across the road.

Dust blew down the street as a small plane circle around overhead, lining up with the road that adjoined the main Oodnadatta track. The hum of a motor flying directly overhead made Jenny realise the aircraft was coming in to land.

Outside the rugged hotel Jenny passed a horse tied up to a post and rail looking hot and bored.

It was after one in the afternoon as she made her way to the pub entrance. Just as she was thinking how quiet the place was, as if on cue, a coach load of tourists pulled up outside and the plane taxied up to park alongside the other light aircraft, opposite the pub.

The bus door opened with a whoosh, the wave of cool air from the air-conditioning a welcomed sensation.

A torrent of tourists, from all walks of life, emptied out of the vehicle, snapping photos and talking excitedly as they swarmed past her, into the hotel.

Sighing, she visualised the bar three rows deep with thirsty tourists. Having no desire to wade through them, she decided to wait to interview the publican. Scanning the concrete path, she considering where she might find a cool and quiet place to wait out the rush.

She caught a glimpse of a tall, broad shouldered figure leaving the back of the pub. He collected the reins of the bored horse and vaulted up into the leather stock saddle without the aid of the stirrup.

'Nick isn't it?' Jenny resisted the urge to jog toward him, but noting the deep laboured breath he drew in before answering.

'It is. You're a long way from home Officer.' Jenny shooed a fly as it tickled her nasal hairs. The corners of Nick's mouth turned up as if the fly had reinforced his statement.

'Not really.' Jenny approached the horse, her hand held out for the animal to sniff. 'How's it going big fella,' she cooed before stroking the chestnut gelding along his muscled neck and flank. His tail flicked in response, or maybe it was to ward off the blowflies that seemed to be attracted to the animal's scent.

'You know horses?' Nick frowned down at her from under his Akubra hat, his blue eyes piercing her with his question.

'I haven't ridden since I was a kid, but I did a lot of it with my cousin.' The thought of Melanie drew Jenny back to why she was out here to begin with. This was her excuse to find out if her cousin and aunt had ever visited the William Creek Station.

The silence between them grew as Jenny shooed yet another sticky fly and Nick's horse stomped with impatience to be on his way. 'I have to talk to the pub owners, but need to wait until this group are settled, so maybe you can help me?'

85

Nick pushed his body into the saddle and the horse backed up. 'I don't have time to stop. I've got work to do.'

'It's just a quick question.' He seemed to hesitate. She took the opening. 'Did you run the William Creek Station about nine years ago?'

'The Station has been in my family for three generations.'

Not an answer. 'So you did?'

'No, my dad did. I was away at University.'

'Oh.' Her hopes of finding information on Melanie were dashed.

'Why?' His horse pranced but Jenny was surprised he wasn't in a hurry to move away now. Curiosity maybe? He waved his hand across his face to shoo a fly. At least they weren't only targeting her. The thought was comforting.

'My aunt and cousin were going to visit the Station, our last name being Williams and all that.' She was waffling. 'Anyway,' she tried to force herself to stop watching his eyes studying her, 'they went missing. I was just hoping if they visited, I could confirm a few missing links in the timeline.'

'Like I said, I wasn't there, but dad kept good records.'

'Oh, that's great.'

'You said they went missing. You mean they never returned home?' Jenny thought she heard concern in his tone.

'No.' *Why was she telling him this?*

'You can email the station their names and approximate dates. I'll do a search.' He didn't wait for any thanks or for any answer at all. He reined his horse around in a half circle and pushed the gelding into a canter.

Jenny watched his comfortable seat on the horse and pushed down a twang of jealously that she was unable to ride out after him. The landscape was hot and arid, but it was teeming with life. It gave off a sense of peace, cathartic, almost spiritual.

She shook her head to clear it, as Nick's outline disappeared into a cloud of red dust. Turning, she pushed open the doors and entered the hotel. Her senses were overwhelmed by the smell of food and beer and the growl of her stomach protesting made her realise she'd driven through lunch.

'I heard that Luv. What can I get you?' A tall woman with fine cheek bones and warm eyes waved from behind the counter.

'Oh, I'm on duty.'

'No reason not to eat luv. Coffee, soft drink?'

'I'll have a non-alcoholic ginger beer thanks.' She stepped up to the bar, her throat suddenly parched. She watched the tourists all huddled around long tables in the next room, their voices creating a hum.

An old billiard table with torn red cloth separated the bar from the dining area and the walls were lined with money, currency notes from all corners of the globe. Signatures of famous people, hats from sporting teams and car racing logos hung from the rafters. The place was a mixture of museum and bar. Jenny could have stayed a month to rummage through the messages from famous people and still not have read them all.

'You're new.' The woman returned with a large glass full of crushed ice and ginger beer.

'That looks awesome.' She took a sip and pulled out her credit card. '

'No luv. On the house.'

'Oh I can't.'

'Yes you can. This is the bush. We do favours, no strings attached, all the time. If I was broken down on the side of the road, I'd like to think you'd offer me a ride and drink with or without the uniform.' The woman's eyes smiled with affection.

'I certainly would.' She returned the smile. 'Thank you.'

'Good for you girl. It's too dangerous out here to stand on silly principles. What brings you out this way?'

'Well, to be honest, a couple of things.' A waitress with an armful of plates glided from behind the bar, out into the restaurant like she'd done it a thousand time. A chicken snitzel laden with gravy, a bowl of pasta as big as a fruit bowl and an inch-thick steak made Jenny's stomach grumble again.

'What can I get you to eat.' It wasn't a question.

Jenny hesitated. 'As long as you let me pay for it,' she grinned.

'You have my word.' The woman nodded solemnly.

'That bowl of pasta looked awesome.' The waitress returned for the next load of plates.

'Get our new Officer a bowl of pasta thanks Jess.'

'On it Mrs B..'

'Mrs B.?'

'You first Luv. You didn't answer my question.' Jenny thought back and realised she hadn't.

'Oh I'm sorry. I got so distracted by the cool drink. It's so hot out there.' Mrs B. waited and Jenny got back on subject. 'I'm new, yes, started this Monday.'

'Where you from?'

'Victor Harbor, south of Adelaide.'

'Oh, lovely spot. How are you going with the boys in Coober Pedy?'

Jenny shrugged. 'They all seem good so far.'

'That's good to hear. What business are you on then?'

The bowl of pasta arrived, likely nicked from the tourist orders. Jenny ignored the guilt and tried not to blush over the preferential treatment. The waitress smiled genuinely as she popped it down on the counter, followed by a fork and spoon a moment later. The aroma wafted into her nostrils making her stomach gurgle in anticipation.

'A few things, like I said.' She pulled the spoon and fork from the paper bag and placed the serviette on the side. 'Tiffany Cox used to work for you. Right?'

'She did. Hard worker too.'

'What happened?' Jenny twirled her fork around the linguini, using the soup spoon to contain the spiral and waited.

'You eat Luv. I'll talk.' Jenny didn't hesitate, the spoonful of pasta was in her mouth before Mrs B. began her story.

'Tiffany was a tough nut. She'd been to hell and back and we believed she had finally found her way forward. But then she reverted to trying to make a little cash on the side.'

Jenny loaded another mouthful on her fork. 'Turning favours you mean?'

'You've heard already.' Jenny nodded, before placing the food in her mouth and savouring it. 'We heard you found her body.'

'News travels fast.' Jenny covered her mouthful of food as she spoke, realising it was probably not polite, but she was hungrier than she thought.

'Bad news always does.' Mrs B. mopped the bar absently. 'Why the questions?'

'Just routine in unexplained deaths.'

'I thought she'd left town.'

'That's what her boyfriend Mark thought too, but obviously not. Why did turning a few tricks on the side cause an issue? Did you sack her for it?'

'No Luv. I'd have never done that but she slept with the wrong guy.'

'What do you mean?' Another mouthful entered Jenny's mouth but she didn't take her eyes from Mrs B..

'Sam Johnston. It was a messy business.' Jenny put her fork down, pulled out her mobile and started to take notes.

'Go on.'

'I shouldn't be telling tales.'

'This is a police investigation Mrs B.. There are no tattle tales.' The woman seemed to consider her a moment.

'She didn't die by accident then?' Jenny opened her mouth to speak. 'I know. It's an ongoing investigation. I wasn't born yesterday luv. I can tell you right now, Sam and Nick have nothing to do with hurting Tiffany but Nick insisted she leave her after he caught her with Sam.'

'Why?'

'Because he's taken on the dad role for his little brother and he does so with an iron fist. Sam had been due to go to university the following March, but when he was caught with Tiffany, he was only sixteen. Nick told her to leave, or he'd press charges.'

'Was Sam paying?'

'No idea, but Tiffany was gutted. I think she was desperate to get in on the William Creek Station fortune if you know what I mean and Nick wouldn't touch her with a barge pole, so Sam was the next best target.'

'But you don't think Nick or Sam would hurt Tiffany?'

'Why would they? She left, shacked up with Mark, then left town. Or so we thought.'

'I have another question.' Jenny put her phone back in her pocket and collected her cutlery again. Loading her fork with a mouthful of linguini, she asked the question she'd been wanting to all along. Not that finding out about Tiffany and the Johnston brothers was a dead end.

'Were you here about nine years ago?'

Mrs B. chuckled. 'Luv, I've been here all my life. Literally. Why?'

Jenny pulled out her phone again. Flicking through her photo album, she brought up a photo of Melanie and her mum together.

'Do you recognise these two women?' Mrs B. took the phone and zoomed in closely to the faces.

'Oh yes. They were hard to forget. The young one, a laugh a minute she was. The bus driver said she flirted with him every second of the trip.'

Jenny kept her expression neutral but the comment didn't surprise her. Melanie was bombshell gorgeous and she was always super popular and very outgoing. Her cousin was the polar opposite of her.

'So they came to the pub here?'

'Yes. Stayed in the bunkhouse out the back. I remember because they checked out in the morning without paying their bill.'

Jenny stopped, her fork hovering in front of her mouth. 'But they'd never do that.'

'How do you know that? Do you know them?'

Chapter 16

Jenny left the pub after fixing up her bill and doing her absolute best not to answer Mrs B.'s question.

She drove into the setting sun for the first half of her trip, until she got back on the Sturt Highway. It was nearly six when she pulled into Coober Pedy. Driving past the station, she found it closed as expected. The day had been a stinker and the crew likely called it early with Len in town.

She needed to get Philips' car back to him, but guessed he'd be in the front bar of the motel with Len and whoever the former local constable's mates were. The only problem was, she wasn't in the mood for socialising.

The answer to her prayers appeared in the shape of Marj.

'Hi Marj.' Jenny greeted the motel manager as she entered reception.

'You look stuffed.'

'I could do with a shower and an early night. Don't suppose you can do me a *huge* favour?'

'Anything for Coober Pedy's finest.' She saluted, a look of mischief twinkled in her eyes.

'I need to get these keys to Danny. I'm guessing he's in the bar with Len. I used his ride today and he'll likely need it to get home tonight.'

'No worries, although I'm not sure either of them will be driving anywhere tonight.' Marj chuckled before turning to leave.

Jenny began to move away, when a thought popped into her head.

'How long ago did Len leave town?' She'd considered the constable must have taken his new job only a week or two before she came, but Sarge had said they'd waited a while for his replacement.

'About six months ago. He got a transfer to somewhere in WA.'

'Nice.' She carried on to her room, wondering why it had taken the station over six months to replace him. Maybe no one wanted to move out here. That was plausible considering she'd only taken the placement for personal reasons.

She opened the door to her room, then realised she still had her duty weapon in her possession. It wasn't protocol to take it home. She was only a constable, but the station wasn't open. She searched the wardrobe, thankful to find a room safe below the chest of drawers. Setting the combination, she took her gun out, checked the safety and put it into the safe, locking it securely away for the night.

After a quick shower, Jenny considered going to the bar for dinner, but she didn't have the energy. Rummaging through her bag, she found a few snacks from the aeroplane flight up. They'd do the trick, tide her over until an early breakfast.

She reached for the file on her missing relatives, then opened a bag of peanuts before dropping onto her bed to read.

A sudden thought made her reach for her laptop before clicking open her email server. A quick Google search revealed the contact information for the William Creek Station and Jenny began typing an email to Nick, hoping he might be able to confirm if her cousin and aunt ever ended up staying there.

She pondered his aloof personality again as she typed. His blue eyes were hard to read. One second his gaze could drill a hole right through her, the next his face said he was ready to throttle someone. Then there were the rare moments when he seemed mildly amused with her. She was going to have to do some digging into Nick Johnston's life and find out more about him. She told herself it was for her investigation as she hit *send* on the email.

Turning back to the police report she noted that the Coober Pedy station had investigated, but found nothing to confirm where Melanie and Aunt Carolyn had stayed. Jenny found that hard to believe and flicked through to find out who'd done the local investigation.

She was surprised to see the Sergeant hadn't signed off on the report, Senior Constable Len had been the investigating officer and he'd signed off on the report as acting head. It was interesting that Len had been Senior and now O'Connell held the position. Did the station have two Seniors or did O'Connell get a promotion once Len left?

Jenny reached for a bag of potato chips, pulled the top open and began to eat, savouring the salty flavour and crunch. The sensation was almost cathartic, relieving her tension better than even a beer.

She yawned and put down the file, deciding to have a casual chat with Len tomorrow if she got the chance. It was fortuitous that he was in town.

****

Tapping on the keyboard to open the case file, Jenny didn't waste any time. 'Bingo.' She said aloud to no one in particular.

'What's up?' O'Connell squinted as his eyes adjusted from the screen to her.

'Tox screen is in on Tiffany.' Jenny opened the file and studied it closely.

'And?'

'Rohypnol.' Philips came into the office as Jenny spoke.

'What's this about?'

'Tiffany. The tox screen shows Rohypnol in her system and,' Jenny scrolled through the document on her screen. 'and she was pregnant.'

'How on earth do they know that?' O'Connell got up and joined Jenny at the computer.

'Hormones in the hair indicate the pregnancy hormone hCG. Lab says she was likely about two to three months pregnant based on hormone levels.'

'And there is no DNA to determine the father so we are going nowhere fast.' O'Connell returned to his chair, leaning back with his hands behind his head.

'How did you go with Mark?' Jenny asked as Philips opened his locker.

'He was beside himself once he found out she was murdered. He hadn't even heard she was found dead yet.' Philips put his backpack away and got out his utility vest.

'How on earth had he not heard yet? It's all over town already and I thought you told him you'd keep him informed if you confirmed anything had happened to her?' Jenny crossed her arms over her chest, suddenly wishing she'd been in on the interview. It was always better if she could see people's faces when questioning them.

'Well it slipped my mind and you saw where he lives. He only comes into town every few weeks for supplies and reception is crap out there.' Philips sounded defensive.

'You do realise that you likely know Tiffany's murderer, don't you?' Her arms were still crossed, her finger now tapping with suppressed irritation.

'Could be a backpacker or someone passing through?'

'That doesn't explain who she was pregnant to. If it wasn't Mark, why hasn't the father of her child come forward to explain their relationship?'

'Maybe he didn't know.' Philips mirrored Jenny's stance.

'Okay you two. We *are* on the same side.' O'Connell interrupted. 'Williams has a point though Philips. We need to stay objective on this. I know it's hard. But over fifty three percent of murders are committed by someone the victim knew.'

'Let's hope Tiffany's murderer was in the other forty-seven percent then.' Philips huffed.

'Big night last night?' Jenny changed the subject.

'Not too huge. Thanks for the keys.'

'No worries. Marj thought you might be too under the weather to drive home.'

'Nah. Len finished up early. Said he had to call home.'

'Domesticated then?' Jenny teased.

'He didn't used to be.' Philips seemed confused by his friend's change in behaviour.

Jenny wanted to raise her question about her family's missing person report, but since Len was involved and Philips appeared ferociously protective of the locals, she decided she'd wait until she could talk with him casually or maybe ask O'Connell what he knew once he was alone.

'Sarge in yet? She peered into the back office, noting the empty desk.

'He's busy.' O'Connell didn't elaborate.

Jenny shrugged it off, but in the back of her mind she wondered about her commanding officer. He was seldom around. He'd not signed off on Len's report about her family. She pushed the thought aside and carried on with Tiffany's case.

'The decomp on the victim indicates she died around June, and since Cheryl said she last saw her at the Festival, we can probably start there.

'When did Mark say she moved out?' O'Connell was jotting down details on a pad at his desk.

'He didn't. But Cheryl confirmed that she knew Tiffany had left Mark when she last saw her at the Festival.' Philips leant against the Senior Constable's desk, watching him make notes.

'So we should start with anyone who likely saw her at the Festival.' Jenny watched Philips and O'Connell exchange glances.

'Nearly everyone in town and in the outer area plus a few thousand tourists were at that festival. How do you propose we do that Williams?' O'Connell was genuinely seeking a solution, but Philips wore a smug grin.

'We put a notice in the paper. We announce it on the local radio station. We use Crime Stoppers in the major cities to call for witnesses.'

'Shit. That means we'll need to get a detective in from Adelaide or Alice.' O'Connell picked up his phone and began to dial.

'Put the phone down O'Connell.' Sergeant Mackenzie stalked in as O'Connell announced his intentions.

'Sir?' O'Connell did as he was told, a frown forming on his brow.

'We aren't calling in the big guns just yet. Give me a report.'

O'Connell gave a quick overview of the details of the case they had so far. The Sergeant listened, nodded, sniffed, even scoffed as the Senior Constable outlined why they needed a detective on deck.

'Look. The way I see it, we still can't rule this a homicide. We have a girl with a questionable reputation, who's fallen down a mine shaft and died. I'm not convinced it wasn't an accident.'

'But the broken hyoid bone?' O'Connell rubbed the back of his neck.

'Could have snapped her neck in the fall.'

'The pregnancy.' Jenny pushed.

'So she got knocked up. She was a slut.'

'Sir!' Jenny knew she sounded defensive. 'What about the missing underwear and drugs in her system?'

'Look Williams. You're new here. You don't know what goes on in this town. I told you there'd be no showboating in my station. Unless the fancy doctors in Adelaide can come up with something more solid, then I'll be steering the Coroner to rule *death by misadventure*.

The Sergeant left the main office for his, closing the door to make it perfectly clear that no one was going to make him change his mind.

Chapter 17

'You heard the boss. Case closed.' O'Connell addressed the two officers in front of him.

'Just like that?' Jenny shook her head. 'Can't I at least question Cheryl again and see if she saw anyone with Tiffany during the Festival?'

'Philips. Head out to Mark, confirm when he last saw Tiffany. Did he see her at the Festival? Once we check that off, we'll close the file until the forensic team come up with something more conclusive.'

Philips left. Jenny's mouth opened and shut twice before she could speak. 'What the hell just happened?'

'The Boss isn't convinced. This is a small-town Williams. I understand his reservations. If we go around accusing the locals of murder, it will stir up a hornet's nest.'

'Sir. If this gets swept under the rug and later something pops up that confirms this is a homicide, then an investigation into misconduct will turn over every stone in this place until they find someone to blame. Surely that will rock the community more than a legitimate murder investigation?'

Jenny couldn't help but wonder if this was what had happened during her aunt and cousin's investigation.

'I hear you, but Sarge has made the call.' O'Connell returned his attention to his keyboard, signalling the end of the conversation.

Maybe now wasn't the time, but Jenny's head was spinning. 'I have an old cold case I'd like your opinion on. If you have a moment.'

'A local one?'

'Sort of.'

'You're being cryptic Williams. Which case?'

'A missing person—actually, two missing people. The report was filed on the South Coast of Adelaide, tracking the subjects to Coober Pedy, but nothing came of it.'

'Why are you chasing this one down?' O'Connell had resumed his earlier position in his chair—leant back, fingers interlaced, hands behind his head.

'It's just that the investigating officer was Senior Constable Len Holmes and Sarge didn't sign off on the report.'

'Tread wisely Williams.' O'Connell's tone spoke volumes.

Jenny pursed her lips, considering her next words carefully. 'The case was nine years ago Sir. A mother and daughter. They sent word—a postcard from Coober Pedy. They had to be here Sir.'

'Nine years ago.' O'Connell checked over his shoulder at the Sergeant's closed door. 'The Boss wasn't doing so well back then. Len was acting station chief at the time.'

'You weren't here?'

'I was. Just not Acting Senior.'

'Is there any chance Len missed something?'

'Why this case Williams?'

It was time to come clean, but could she trust O'Connell? More importantly, would he be pissed off with her and send her home?

'Can we keep this between you and me Sir?'

'For now.' O'Connell leant forward and Jenny stepped closer to his desk.

'The two missing women were my cousin Melanie and my auntie Carolyn Williams.'

'Geez Williams. That's why you took this placement?'

'Yes Sir. But don't get me wrong. Working each case that crosses my desk is my priority.'

'I can see that by the way you pushed Sergeant Mackenzie in Tiffany's case, but you need to tread lightly girl.'

'Why?'

'Sarge was still grieving nine years ago. Let's say a lot went right by him back then. We covered for him as best we could. He's all good now. Tough nugget.'

'Is this about his daughter's death?'

O'Connell nodded. 'Len took on a huge workload back then. It was just us three, before Philips' time.'

'I understand Sir. I'll keep it discreet, but I already discovered that my relatives stayed at the William Creek Pub, but skipped out unexpectedly. They wouldn't have done that by choice Sir.'

'Damn. What a mess.'

'Sir, can I speak with Cheryl again? Just to make sure we haven't missed anything?'

O'Connell took a deep breath that made his nostrils flare. He ran his hand through his thick mop of salt and pepper hair and sighed again. He didn't say a word, but a quick, curt nod of his head gave her the all clear.

She didn't wait for him to change his mind.

Ten minutes later she was sitting with Cheryl Peterson, drinking a coffee in the paved outdoor area outside the motel restaurant. Grape vines grew over a pergola that kept the sun from heating up the area, but it was still warmer than Jenny liked.

'Cheryl. We need to piece together Tiffany's movements during the Opal Festival. You said you last saw her there.'

'Yeah. She was a bit scatter-brained. We were supposed to meet up for food before the Priscilla Queen of the Desert tribute show came on, but she was late.'

'What time was that?'

101

'About seven.'

'She told Mark she was leaving him for a rich guy and they were heading out of town. Any idea who she was talking about?'

'Why are you asking these questions? Didn't Tiffany fall down the mine?'

'We don't know for sure yet Cheryl. This is just routine. We are trying to piece together her last movements. Do *you* think she fell into the mine?'

'I don't know.' Cheryl looked away, then her eyes dropped to her hands, fidgeting in her lap. She hadn't touched her coffee.

'Take a sip of coffee and a deep breath. Give yourself time to think.' Cheryl put her finger through the cup handle, lifting it slowly to her lips and swallowed a mouthful.

'Tiff had been acting weird since she left Mark. She said she left because of the dark, damp mine, but I think she could have been seeing someone.'

'Do you know who?'

'I got the impression he was married. That's all I could work out from what she said.'

'What did she say?' Jenny waited, trying not to look too eager or point out that Cheryl had already said she didn't know Tiffany was seeing someone. This could be what she'd been looking for. The father of Tiffany's baby.

'It was more what she didn't say. When I asked her what was going on—was she seeing someone? She looked guilty. If she was seeing someone she was supposed to be dating, she would have just said yes.' Cheryl's eyes were begging for an answer. 'Wouldn't she?'

'It makes sense, but you don't know who?' She shook her head. 'Do you remember what you did after the Priscilla show?'

'We hung out for an hour or so. She was pretty distracted and it didn't take long for her to make an excuse to wriggle away.'

'Which direction did she go?'

Cheryl turned her cup full circle, then lifted it to her lips for another sip, her eyebrows creased with concentration. 'She went toward the emergency services tents. The ambulance, fire fighters, S.E.S., that crew.'

Jenny made notes on her phone. 'That's great Cheryl.' She sculled her coffee. 'Let me know if you remember seeing her again, or anything strange happening that night.' She got up to leave.

'I did see something else, but I'm not sure I saw it clearly.' She put her hand on top of Jenny's arm, preventing her from leaving. The action held a sense of desperation, even fear.

'It was the emergency service tent she went towards, so it wasn't as though it didn't make sense.'

'What did you see?'

'Just as the fireworks were announced, I saw Tiffany near the tents again. I'm sure it was her, but I couldn't make out the guy with her. He wore a uniform. I'm just not sure which type. It was dark.'

Jenny's mind was racing. 'How do you know it was a uniform then?'

'There were reflective panels on the shoulders.'

'That's extremely helpful.'

'I wish I'd seen more, but like I said, it was dark.'

'It's okay Cheryl. We are just piecing together her last movements, trying to find out why she went to the mines that night, or maybe she went home and the mine accident was a different day. That type of thing.'

'I never saw her again. I would have seen her if she'd been alive after that night.' Jenny could see the pain in Cheryl's eyes. 'I should have stayed with her. Why would she go Noodling at night like that?'

'Maybe whoever was with her encouraged her?' Jenny tapped Cheryl's hand and the woman let her arm go, suddenly realising she'd kept a hold of it all that time.

'I'm sorry,' she mumbled.

'Don't be. She was your friend and you went through a lot together.' She considered her next question carefully. Was it necessary to the investigation? Maybe, considering where Tiffany's body had been discovered.

'It must have been tough after Jacob died?'

Cheryl's eyes darted to Jenny's, a look of fear and anger mixed together in a volatile cocktail.

'We never talked about it. Ever!'

'Forget I mentioned it then. Let me know if you think of anything else that might help work out where Tiffany went after the Festival.'

Cheryl said nothing, but Jenny wasn't hanging around to see if the girl had calmed down. The look she'd given her sent shivers down her spine. Jacob Henderson must have been one nasty piece of work.

The thought that maybe he didn't commit suicide crossed her mind again, but she had enough unsolved cases to keep her occupied without worrying about how a deadhead like Jacob had died. The little voice in her head that told her *everyone deserved justice,* got told in no uncertain terms to *shut up!*

Who would have been at the tents Cheryl described? With a reflective uniform? Tim possibly. The ambulance officers would have been on duty in case of an accident. They had reflective panels on their uniforms so they didn't get hit by traffic.

Jenny had researched the Opal Festival and discovered it was the biggest show of the year, with rides, sideshows, stalls, food, BMX bike races, a huge parade and live entertainment to keep the masses engaged.

The ambulance, S.E.S., fire service and even the police would have all been in the parade. Someone must have seen something, but her questioning was going to come to an abrupt standstill if she couldn't prove Tiffany was murdered.

Jenny pulled her mobile phone from her pocket and made a call.

Chapter 18

'Penny. Sorry to bug you.' Jenny watched Marj walk by towards the rear of the restaurant. She waved, then ducked around the back to ensure Marj couldn't eavesdrop.

'Not at all. I was just about to call your station.'

'Why? What have you found?' Jenny glanced over her shoulder. Marj loved town gossip. The last thing she needed was for the motel owner to overhear anything.

'Fibres on the victim's body that are inconsistent with her own clothing.'

'Fibres? Like someone else's clothing?'

'Yep. I've checked and double checked this Jenny. The fibres came from an SA ambulance uniform.' There was a moment of silence as Jenny absorbed the data. 'You still there?'

'Yeah, sorry. I just got information from Tiffany's closest friend that she saw her leave the Festival with someone wearing a uniform, with reflective panels on it.'

'A paramedic?'

'Possibly. We need to investigate this further, but Sergeant Mackenzie is pushing the coroner to rule it death by misadventure.'

'No way.'

'Anything you can do Penny?'

'Sure. I'll pass on my findings to Doc Holbrook and insist that the local cops consider at least the idea that she was accidentally pushed or someone saw it happen and failed to render assistance. I can't believe with the signs pointing to sexual assault your Sergeant isn't treating this as a suspicious death.'

'Me neither. Something isn't right about any of this. Sarge is dead against bringing in a detective to investigate a possible murder, but I don't want to go over his head. I've only been here less than a week.'

'I get ya. Don't worry. I'll do what I can my end.'

'I appreciate it.'

'No problem. I saw the scene remember and I've analysed her clothing. She wasn't dressed for fossicking. With a broken hyoid bone, the missing knickers, the toxicology report and now foreign fibres, not to mention the fact no one reported her missing—it all points to murder as far as I can see, but the push to investigate needs to come from the local station unless Doc can be certain it's homicide.'

'I'll keep digging and see what we can do.'

'Jenny.' There was tension in Penny's voice.

'Yeah?'

'Be careful. If the locals don't want to push, you have to wonder why.'

'Yeah. I've been thinking the same thing.'

Jenny hung up, put her phone in her pocket and headed back to the station to fill out a report on her interview with Cheryl.

Len was standing by the doorway as she approached, a smoke hanging out of his mouth. He watched her draw closer, his expression a mixture of contemplation and forced politeness.

'Williams,' he nodded as she passed by.

Jenny could feel his eyes on her retreating back. Being a female police officer, that was nothing new. She'd become aware years ago that female cops seemed to fill just about every boy's wet dream and she knew, that although she was plain, she wasn't ugly.

'Williams!' Jenny jumped at the intensity of Sergeant Mackenzie's voice.

'Yes Sir?'

'My office.' Jenny glanced at O'Connell, her eyebrow raised. His expression was kind, but he only offered her a shrug. She scanned the room for Philips. He must have still been out questioning Mark.

There was no one else to offer her moral support. She drew her shoulders back and told herself she didn't need it. She didn't expect any favours when she came to Coober Pedy. She had one main goal, well two now that she had Tiffany's case on her hands, but she knew she'd endure anything to find out what happened to her cousin and aunt.

'Close the door.' Jenny did as she was told, taking the seat the Sergeant indicated opposite his desk.

He sat in his chair, a whoosh of air released as his heavier frame sank back. He didn't speak immediately, which further unnerved Jenny. Surely Penny hadn't managed to get the Coroner to act already?

'Why are you here Williams?'

'Sir?' Her trust in O'Connell might have been misplaced.

'You have to stop going off book Williams.'

'I don't understand Sir? You mean interviewing Cheryl again? I was just finalising the investigation so we can submit a full and concise report.'

'Don't give me that shit. You're trying to make a name for yourself and using the Coober Pedy community as a ladder rung to get you there. That isn't okay with me Constable.' Sarge's eyes were greyer than usual. He looked beat, like he'd aged since even the day before.

'I'm not interested in anything but finding out the truth Sir. I thought that's what the police did—at least they did where I came from.' Jenny knew her tone was disrespectful of her commanding officer, but he was being a wanker.

'Williams. I gave you an order to *drop* this case.'

'I'm just tying up loose ends. I don't see anything wrong with that.'

'Is that what you call it?

'Sir. Tiffany was seen leaving the Opal Festival with a man. That night was the last night she was seen alive. At the very least, the guy could tell us where she went and how she ended up down a mine, with a broken hyoid bone, wearing her best clothing and sandals and minus her underwear.'

Sarge stared at her face, as though he were seeing her for the first time. She knew her face was flushed and the heat rash that invaded her chest and neck when she was nervous or angry was working overtime.

'Have you even read the notes Sir?' Controlling her anger was never easy – the result of the little tinge of red in her otherwise brown hair. At least the Scottish heritage was her excuse and she was sticking to it. It seemed Sergeant Mackenzie might possess the same Scottish blood.

'Don't use that tone with me Constable. I'll have your badge in a heartbeat.'

'I've done nothing wrong Sir.' The tone was now a whine.

'I'm watching you Williams.'

Jenny wanted to ask the Sergeant where *he* was the night Tiffany went missing. Was he the married man she was dating? None of this was making any sense. Why didn't he want to get to the bottom of Tiffany's death?

'Is that all Sir?' There was a long, painful silence before Jenny decided she should just leave. Standing, she tried unsuccessfully not to stomp her way to the door.

'You don't know this place Williams.' She turned back to watch her Sergeant carefully. Was it a threat? Was it a warning?

'I will Sir. You have my word on it.' Jenny opened the office door and stormed out. She didn't look at O'Connell, at least the guy hadn't told Sarge about her personal agenda.

'I'm going for lunch since the Tiffany case is closed!' She stormed out of the office, past Len who was loitering outside. He chuckled as she rushed by.

'Piss off Holmes.' She didn't look at him. She was fuming and he was just a leering dickhead.

All the testosterone was making her head spin. She wanted to talk to Tim but she needed to be careful. If an ambulance officer was with Tiffany that night, it could have been Tim, or one of his mates. How to interview him without actually making it look like an interview?

Chapter 19

Jenny didn't have a car. She didn't have Tim's phone number either, just Nev's. Maybe she could start with him? He was probably there that night too. It seemed the whole town went to the Opal Festival.

She pulled her mobile out and sent a text. *Nev, are you free for a chat?*

Doctors carried their mobiles on them all the time. She didn't have to wait long for a response.

Anything wrong?

No. Just the boys at the station are giving me the shits.

I'm on break in 30. Where?

No strings okay?

Okay, (laughing face emoji), *just mates catching up.*

The motel restaurant? I don't have wheels.

See you in 30.

Thanks. She started to type a heart emoji but decided she was trying *not* to give Nev the wrong impression and although hearts between female friends were common, they were unadvisable in this case.

Jenny crossed the road, the dust lifting in the still air with every step she took. The sun belted down, making sweat run down her back. She wondered how anyone got used to the dry heat of this place. Maybe they didn't. Maybe they just learned to live with it.

There were a few scattered native shrubs here and there in town. The undertone of green-grey foliage competed with the remaining landscape of multi-coloured sands spreading as far as the eye could see. The barren landscape seemed to reflect her mood in that moment.

Sighing, she opened the glass door to a wave of cool air that made her skin tingle with anticipation of standing in front of the full force of the air-conditioning vent. The hum of voices from the front bar filtered through to the restaurant as miners called it an early day and chased a cold beer to refresh themselves.

Jenny checked her watch, realising it was later than she thought.

'What will you have Officer?'

'Just a non-alcoholic ginger beer thanks Stan.' It was only Friday of her first week and Jenny was already settling in as a regular in this little restaurant. 'I'm on duty still.'

'That never stopped your predecessor.' He shrugged like it shouldn't stop her either, but Jenny wasn't about to cross that line.

The idea that Len Holmes drank on the job didn't surprise her, but it made her think of her Sergeant and what O'Connell said about him when his daughter died. Alcohol was his crutch. Was he still married? Was he still an alcoholic?

'You having lunch?'

'Yes thanks.' Stan handed her a menu which she took, with her drink to a table around the corner from the bar. The place was large, with a central bar where a lot of the locals milled after work.

To the left was an expansive restaurant, used mostly for the breakfast buffet and big nights of entertainment like the Karaoke night she'd experienced on arrival. To the right was a smaller seating area, suitable for more intimate conversation. It led out to the paved courtyard she'd met Cheryl in earlier. Overall, the building was far bigger than the small motel could need for guests, but it was one of the two or three meeting places for the locals.

It was said Australia had a pub on every corner, and this was living proof the saying wasn't far from true.

'Did you order yet?' Nev pulled out the chair next to her.

'No. Haven't even checked out the menu to be honest.' She'd been off with the fairies, thinking about Tiffany and O'Connell and Sergeant Mackenzie and Len and even how many pubs were in Coober Pedy. Oh how her head was spinning.

'You look worse than an intern after a forty-eight-hour straight shift.'

'You say the nicest things. I've got a lot on my plate.'

'This is Coober Pedy Jenny. You can't have that much going on.'

'It's complicated.'

'You said the boys were annoying you. What's up?'

'Len Holmes. What do you know about him?'

'Food first, then gossip.'

'Gossip?'

'What are you having?' Nev grabbed the menu and skimmed it without taking it in. He'd eaten there often enough to already know exactly what he wanted. His choice made, he handed it back.

'I'm going a steak with béarnaise sauce.'

'For lunch!' Jenny's eyes were wide.

'I've been busy and I have to cover someone's shift tonight, so I probably won't get dinner anyway.'

Jenny checked the menu over quickly. She was hungry. She'd missed dinner last night and eaten breakfast in a hurry, but she reminded herself you couldn't exactly make up for missed meals in one sitting. Either way, her stomach told her it was worth a try.

'Okay. I'll have the lasagne with chips and salad.'

'You go girl. Carbs are your friend.'

'What's that supposed to mean?'

'Nothing. I know lots of girls who can't eat them. They go straight to their thighs but you can eat whatever you want, can't you?'

Jenny considered the statement. 'Yeah, and I love pasta. My mum was forced to stop eating it when she got older, so I'm making the most of it in case I have the same issue.'

Nev laughed. 'I'll be back in a second.'

'Hey. I didn't invite you here to shout me lunch.'

'My buy, yours next time. Besides, you got the kebabs.'

'True.'

A few minutes later, Nev was back at the table, a light beer in hand. Jenny wondered if drinking while working as a doctor was sensible, but she said nothing.

'So you want gossip on your predecessor?'

'I just wondered about a few things.'

'Len's a little old school. But he gets the job done.'

'Meaning?'

'He knocked a few heads in his time.'

'All above board though?'

Nev shrugged. 'I've only been here five years. He apparently held the reins in the station for a while, before my time.'

'Yeah, I heard about Sarge's daughter's accident. Is he married?'

'Who, Sergeant Mackenzie or Len?'

'Sarge? I heard Len is.'

'Sergeant Mac's wife left after the accident.'

'That's sad.'

'It's a lot for any marriage to withstand, but word is they'd been breaking apart before their daughter's death.'

'And Len's wife?'

'His wife is a ball breaker. Seriously. Only met her a few times but she scared the crap out of me.'

'That's weird. He doesn't strike me as the type to be under the thumb.'

'You'd be surprised.'

'Did you go to the Opal Festival last year?'

'Sure. Everyone went. I was on shift in the hospital through most of the day, but I managed to get to the evening entertainment and fireworks.'

A buzzer went off on the table, indicating their meals were ready to pick up.

'I've got it.' Nev got up, took his now empty glass back to the bar and ordered a refill as he went to the servery and collected their meals. He expertly juggled both plates on one arm like he'd worked as a waiter, while picking up the now replenished beer.

'Aren't you on duty?' Jenny quizzed as Nev sat down and put her meal in front of her.

'I am, but I'll burn this off in thirty minutes of running around the wards in the hospital. We don't have a lot of staff. I cover a load of patients and beds.'

'Sorry, none of my business.' Jenny took a sip of her own drink and collected up the cutlery to start on her lasagne.

'All good. Why did you ask about the Festival?'

Jenny glanced up from her food, the thought of whether to ask Nev any more questions bounced around her head a moment too long.

'Is this about Tiffany?'

'Sort of.'

'Are you making an official enquiry?' Nev frowned, his hands poised to consume his medium-rare T-Bone steak.

'No. Definitely not. I'm just trying to piece together a few things. Totally *un*official.' She wasn't lying. Sarge warned her off the case, but she couldn't let it go. Something in her heart told her Tiffany was murdered and the fact that no one seemed concerned was pissing her off.

'So what do you need to know?' Nev filled his fork and started eating, obviously convinced Jenny didn't see him as a suspect in anything untoward.

'Tiffany was last seen leaving the emergency service tents with someone that wore a uniform, with reflective panels on it.'

'So ambo, S.E.S. or firey.'

'That was my assumption.' She kept the knowledge Penny shared to herself. So far, there was no guarantee the person Tiffany left with was the same one whose uniform fibres were found on the body. 'I'd like to ask Tim if he saw her that night but I don't want him to think I'm trying to pin anything on him.'

'Don't be silly. He's cool. He was on shift that night, for sure, but so were a load of the local crew. Then there were the volunteers.'

'Volunteers?' Jenny put another fork load of lasagne in her mouth.

'Yeah. The paid ambulance crew couldn't cover the whole event. S.E.S is mostly made up of volunteers all trained in first aid. Quite a few would have donned the ambo green to help out for the night.'

'So with the S.E.S. volunteers and the country fire service, there were a lot of volunteers wearing uniforms with high vis panels.'

'Exactly.'

'So I'm still no closer to finding out who was the last person to see Tiffany alive.'

'Here. This is Tim's number. Give him a call.' Jenny's phone pinged with a contact file for Tim. 'He'll have a list of all the rostered ambulance volunteers. He'll also know who to talk to with the S.E.S. and C.F.S. to put a list of volunteers together from them too.'

'Thanks Nev. That's a great help.' Jenny finally took another mouthful of her food as ideas began running around her head. These lists would give her a load of people to interview. She'd need to narrow it down so she didn't alert her boss what she was up to.

But how on earth was she going to do that?

Chapter 20

Jenny dialled Tim's number as she left the restaurant. It rang three times before going to voicemail. 'Tim, it's Jenny, Constable Jenny.' She couldn't explain why she clarified who she was. How many Jennys did Tim know?

'I need a favour if you have a few minutes. Give me a call. Thanks.'

She hung up and made her way over the road back to the station. O'Connell looked up from his desk as she entered.

He watched her move around the back of the counter. 'Have I got food on my face or something?' She joked, but O'connell wasn't smiling.

'The Boss is looking for you and he doesn't sound happy.' O'Connell nodded toward the back of the station.

Jenny wanted to say *what's new*, but held her tongue. The Sergeant appeared in his office doorway, one arm resting on the frame, the other on his hip, his finger tapping his belt.

'Williams.' He stepped aside and indicated with his thumb for her to join him. She watched his expression closely as he stepped aside, allowing her room to enter. His face was calm, his shoulders slumped. None the less, she braced for another lecture.

'Close the door.' *Not again.* Jenny followed his instructions, before joining him at his desk and taking the seat she'd come to believe was built for interrogation, not comfort.

'I got a call from the Coroner's office. Apparently, they won't sign off on Death by Misadventure.' He'd taken a seat and was sitting back now, his hands clasped together, his thumbs dancing on the top like he couldn't keep them still.

Jenny opted to remain silent, while her boss studied her closely. 'The forensic scientist who examined the scene has interceded. Do you know anything about that?' His tone was still calm. Jenny thought that was a good sign. Then she recalled her friend's dad and how he used to always go quiet when he was extremely angry. They called it *the calm before the storm.*

'She seemed thorough and professional when she was here Sir. I guess she found something of interest.' Jenny wasn't giving anything away. Mackenzie was quiet a moment.

'Fibres, but you already knew that, didn't you?'

Jenny chose not to answer. How could he know she knew?

'The Coroner's office isn't calling it homicide, but they are asking for us to investigate further.'

'Yes Sir.'

'A Doctor Holbrook has advised there is enough evidence to suggest that the victim was in an altercation before her death and that only the lack of physical evidence due to the level of decomposition is the reason he isn't ruling it a murder investigation.'

Jenny watched the Sergeant closely. *Why was he telling her this?*

'Coober Pedy is a small-town Williams.' Jenny waited, wondering where this was going. His tone remained calm, almost apologetic and she could see by his posture he was tired. 'I want you to tread very carefully as you carry on with this investigation.'

'You want me to look into it? Why not Philips or O'Connell?'

'Because you're new, with fresh eyes.'

Jenny saw Mackenzie's eyes flicker. Frowning, she let the cogs tumble around her head, considering what motivated the sudden change of heart. 'And if I upset anyone, or stuff up, you can hang me out to dry.' Mackenzie stared at her a

119

moment, then a curve of his lips told her she'd hit the nail right on the head.

'You're quick Williams.'

'I'll take that as a compliment.'

'Good. I haven't seen your level of vigour for a while and I'll be honest, it scared the shit out of me when I first saw you....But, if someone did in fact help Tiffany leave this world, we need to know who and how.'

Jenny waited a moment, being careful not to ruin the Sergeant's good mood. 'Sir, can I ask you a question?'

The Sergeant studied her thoughtfully, then nodded.

'Why were you so willing to believe she'd just fallen?'

He sucked in a breath and puffed his cheeks out. She watched as he considered her question. His faced moved through a myriad of emotions. A frown, an eyebrow lift, a shake of the head. Finally, he shrugged, relaxed and fixed his eyes on hers.

'I've been at this job a while Williams. Just between you and me, I'm getting tired of the crap that goes on in people's lives. This place is isolated and the people who are here are most often here because they have to be, or because they are addicted to the mining and the lure of that big find. Part of me figured that Tiffany should have left town years ago and that her death was her own responsibility, but that's not how it should be.'

Jenny didn't know what to say. How could it ever have been Tiffany's fault she was dead? Sure, she should have left town, but she was a victim many years before she was killed.

'Why have you stayed Sir?' The question popped out and Jenny threw her hand over her mouth too late.

Mackenzie smiled at her. 'You remind me of my daughter Williams. Maybe another reason why I was such a cranky arsehole when you arrived. She was always giving me lip. Tread carefully—this place is often not what it seems to be.' He nodded toward the door.

Jenny got up to leave, the discussion obviously over and she knew she wasn't getting an answer to her question.

'Williams, make sure you look like I've dragged you through the coals again. I don't want Philips or O'Connell getting the idea I've left you on this case. Not yet anyway.'

Jenny nodded, but wondered why on earth the Sergeant would want to keep an open investigation from the team.

'Yes Sir.' She opened the door as the answer hit her. He wanted complete deniability. He could tell head office she was on the case, but tell the locals she was acting off book. Or maybe he'd tell head office she was rogue. Her stomach rolled as she realised she was walking a tight-rope and any step could be her last. She needed to keep her wits about her, or she could lose her only chance of finding out what happened to her cousin and aunt.

Her mobile buzzed in her pocket as she approached the front desk, answering, she slunk past the counter, out of the main office area for privacy.

'Tim.'

'Jenny. Got your message. What do you need?'

'I'm sorry to bother you, but can I get a copy of the volunteer roster for the night of the Opal Festival, plus do you know the S.E.S. and Country Fire Service contacts so I can get their rosters too?'

'Sure. It will take me a few hours to dig it out of my computer files. I'll text you Joe and Jeff's contact info. Joe handles the S.E.S and Jeff the C.F.S.'

'Okay great, thanks for that.'

'Jenny, what's this about?' Tim sounded pensive, even a little nervous.

Jenny rubbed her chin as she considered how much she should be trusting Tim. Maybe he wasn't as innocent as she believed. 'It's just routine Tim.'

There was a moment of silence and Jenny knew Tim wasn't buying her explanation but he must have decided not to push it. 'I'll get onto it as soon as I get back to the office.'

'Thanks Tim. Nev said you'd be all good with it.'

'Yeah.' His tone said he wasn't. 'See ya.'

'Bye.' Jenny hung up and took a slow breath as she planned her next move. What she'd rather do was hand the case over to a detective from Adelaide or Alice Springs, but the Sergeant wasn't going to do that any time soon.

Jenny opened the station door to go back inside. She wanted to find out how Philips' interview with Mark went. Had he seen Tiffany the night of the Opal Festival? But how was she going to quiz him without the rest of the team finding out she was still investigating Tiffany's death?

Her mind was overloaded with thoughts, making it difficult to breathe. Transferring into the Boondocks was a sacrifice she was willing to make to find out what happened to her family but now she was so invested in discovering who killed Tiffany, her family investigation was going to have to wait.

Philips pulled up in the police Landcrusier as Jenny entered the station. She peered back through the glass doors, noticing Len getting out of the passenger's side. She couldn't help but wonder why the Senior Constable was going on call-outs with Philips when he was off duty, but she kept her curiosity to herself.

'Williams.' O'Connell watched her lift the countertop and enter the main office. 'You okay?'

'I'll live.' Jenny moved to the computer at the main counter and began collating Tiffany's file, opening the reports that Penny sent through. Philips entered with Len, their good-natured banter setting her on edge—mainly because Len was staring at her, even though it was Philips talking to him.

'Get anywhere with Mark?' Fortunately O'Connell asked the question Jenny couldn't.

'I'll get to the report Sir, sorry. I've been busy.' He glanced over at Len. Jenny wondered why. For moral support maybe?

'Well tell me the details now, then write up your report, from Mark's interview and the earlier domestic. Paperwork Philips. Love it or hate it, it has to be done.'

'Yes Sir. Mark didn't go to the Opal Festival. Said he drank too much, still upset over Tiffany leaving.'

'That's not much of an alibi.' O'Connell offered. 'Anyone else with him?'

'No Sir.'

'Alibi? Why does he need an alibi? I thought Sarge wasn't pursuing homicide?' Len asked too casually. Jenny watched his expression carefully as O'Connell frowned at Philips. Len hadn't been in the station when Sarge called them off the case.

'He's the last known partner of a dead girl. Just crossing off the 'T's' Len.' O'Connell stared at Philips and the constable visibly cringed. He knew he shouldn't be sharing an ongoing case with anyone outside the station, even a police officer from another jurisdiction, but Jenny couldn't exactly judge him. She'd told Nev way too much already.

O'Connell locked eyes with her. She averted his scrutinising stare. He knew she was still on the case. He must know. He was feeding her the information she needed. What she wasn't sure about was if he knew Sarge put her onto it, or he just realised she wasn't the type to give up easily, even if ordered off.

Chapter 21

Jenny sat on her bed, wishing there was a desk in the small motel room and wondering if she was supposed to live here for her entire career in the bush. Was finding her own place to call home an option? She was so snowed under with Tiffany's case that she hadn't taken in the local town or tourist sights.

The thought reminded her that the weekend was just around the corner and she'd have plenty of time to check out the local highlights and discover more about Coober Pedy soon.

She opened her email account and found a reply from the William Creek Station. She couldn't explain it, but butterflies fluttered in her stomach as she opened it. Was she apprehensive over discovering more about her cousin and aunt or was it hearing back from Nick that made her nervous?

The latter didn't make any sense. The guy was good looking but he was a rude arse and hadn't exactly endeared himself to her since they'd met. So why couldn't she get his crystal blue eyes out of her head?

She read the email and rubbed her temples, allowing her mind to digest the contents. Melanie and Aunt Carolyn booked in to take the horse trail expedition but according to Nick's father's records, they'd never showed up.

'Damn.' It wasn't the answer she'd hoped for. She knew she was pushing it, especially since Nick was less than friendly, but maybe, just maybe she could head out and talk with some of the workers who might have been there while Nick was away at university. She began typing a reply.

Thanks so much for checking for me. I was thinking that maybe one of the staff might have seen my cousin and aunt, at the pub maybe before they went missing. Is there any chance I can come out to meet them? Show my cousin's photo around? Please! It would mean a lot to know who might have seen them last and where?

She hit the *send* button not expecting anything to come of it. Nick seemed to be extremely inhospitable. She thought about his brother. Maybe Sam would be more helpful, but he was so young. He'd have been only eight or nine when her cousin visited. Still, it was worth a shot. She'd ask around and discover where to find Sam. Or maybe Mick, his mum was Mrs B., maybe Mick would remember something.

She scanned her email once more, hoping to find the list from Tim, then remembered he would have sent it to her work email. She needed to follow up on the S.E.S and C.F.S. contact details too. This was still official police business even if she wasn't supposed to tell O'Connell or Philips, so using her personal email or calling after hours was unprofessional.

Sighing, she accepted there was nothing more she could do tonight on either case. Closing her computer down, she pulled her work uniform off, dumping it on the floor on her way to the bathroom to run a shower.

The rest of her personal items were yet to arrive. Not that she owned much, only a few boxes and suitcases of clothing to come, but still, she was unsettled—like she was on some horrific holiday in the middle of nowhere, with no one she knew and her luggage was lost.

The steam drifted from the bathroom, telling her it was time to jump in the shower. Her hair was long and washing it at night was a huge mistake, especially without a blow dryer, but nearly a week's worth of dust had settled on her scalp, leaving her no choice.

Ten minutes later she was wringing the water out of her auburn locks and tying it up in a loose bun, hoping it wouldn't drip on her clothing. Her arms were slow to move, as though rocks were tied to her fingers. Her stomach gurgled as her eyes fell on the kettle and toaster above the bar fridge that rattled beneath. A cup of noodles wasn't going to cut it tonight. The restaurant in the motel was her only hope of a meal.

She scanned the courtyard as she locked her door. Goose bumps covered her skin, but nothing caught her eye as dangerous. Cautiously, she walked down the covered walkway toward the dining room. The night was warm, the temperature from the heated earth radiated up from the ground, but still, a shiver ran down her spine.

She resisted the urge to look over her shoulder, instead she picked up pace, keeping her senses alert. Reaching for her gun, she reminded herself she was off duty and her weapon was securely packed away in the gun safe at the station.

Two guys left the restaurant. Jenny hurried through the open door, her heart racing. She told herself she was over-reacting, but as the double glass doors closed behind her, she noticed a stocky figure silhouetted against the courtyard floodlights.

Was it her imagination, or was someone trying to intimidate her into backing off Tiffany's case, or… was it her cousin and aunt's case that was making someone nervous? She tried to convince herself it was probably nothing, but her gut tumbled into knots.

'Hey. Did you get my email?' Jenny spun around at the sound of Tim's voice. He studied her face, then frowned. 'Are you okay?' He stepped forward, watching her carefully.

'I'm fine thanks Tim.' She put her hand up to set his mind at ease. It was shaking. 'It's just been a late one, that's all.' Tim held her eyes a moment, searching for more. After a few agonising seconds, he nodded.

'In that case, I'll get you a beer.'

'That would be awesome, thanks Tim.' Jenny followed him to the bar. 'What time did you send the email?'

'Last thing before I left the office.'

'I'll probably see it tomorrow. I need to chase up the other guys, but I'll get onto it.'

'Working Saturdays?'

Jenny shrugged. 'It seems the hours are flexi-time here in the bush. I should get off by lunch, fingers crossed.'

'This is about Tiffany isn't it? Nev told me.' Jenny smiled, the bush telegraph was working overtime. 'You think she was murdered?'

'I can't comment on an ongoing case Tim, but at this stage, we are just making sure we've got a complete picture of her final movements.'

'I get it. She was a nice chick and it's a real shame she's dead but you can't seriously think someone local killed her?' He handed her a beer and Jenny turned to find a seat.

'I need to grab some dinner Tim. You're welcome to join me. I've actually got another favour to ask, nothing to do with Tiffany this time.' Jenny stopped and grabbed a menu from the bar before moving to take a seat. She knew only a handful of people in town and the last thing she wanted to do was isolate Tim. Penny thought he was alright, so he probably was and she needed all the friends she could find. Especially now that Sarge wanted her digging into this case behind Philips' and O'Connell's back.

'What favour?' Tim took a long draw of his beer and fiddled with the cardboard coaster on the table before placing it under his glass, the condensation running down the side like rain on a windscreen.

She'd been thinking about Nick but when his email arrived, there was something niggling at the back of her mind about him and the way he gave her such a cold shoulder when they first met. Everyone said she resembled her cousin Melanie, except taller and lankier. She couldn't help but wonder if Nick met Melanie all those years ago after all.

'Do you know much about Nick Johnston?' Tim grinned and Jenny realised what he was thinking. 'Nothing like that. I've only met him twice and each time he's been a real grump.'

'All I know is rumour. I wasn't here when it happened but Nick cut his university study short and return to the station to look after his little brother Sam.'

'What happened?' She suddenly realised this might be why Nick was so protective of Sam. Mrs B. inferred as much.

'His mum disappeared, but not before his dad was found with his head blown off.'

'No way!'

'Yep. You could probably find out more than me about it from the police report, but it was ruled suicide.'

'That's horrible.' She was going to say he never mentioned anything but why would he? Suicide was not something that came up in general conversation but it explained a lot about why he was so aloof. Jenny couldn't help seeing his clear blue eyes in her mind. Had she mistaken pain for indifference?

Chapter 22

'Williams, you and Philips need to check out a disturbance at the old Mallory mine.'

Jenny glanced up from the main computer, hit send on an email to Joe and Jeff about their rosters for the festival and opened Tim's list. 'Sure boss. I just need to print something off.' O'Connell nodded as Philips pulled his gun out of the safe, checked it and placed it in his holster.

She hit *print* on Tim's list, shut the document and left the computer to collect her weapon. Passing the printer on the way, she stopped, picked up the list and placed it into Tiffany's case folder.

O'Connell watched her closely as she loaded her weapon, checked it out and holstered it. Placing Tiffany's case folder into a tray on the front counter, she hoped he wasn't interested enough to read the print out. If he did, there shouldn't be an issue. It was just a list and he likely wouldn't know what it was about without her notes to go with it.

'Where is the old Mallory mine?' she asked as Philips held the door for her. The wave of heat that greeted her was vicious, only feeding the thought that she'd never get used to the extreme temperatures. The whole area was majestic one minute, torturous the next. She couldn't help but notice the ripple of heat haze that hovered over the landscape as she opened the door of the Landcruiser.

'It's just out west near the golf club.'

'The golf club. Coober Pedy has a golf club?'

'Sure we do.' Philips gave her an indignant look.

'But you can't grow grass out here, can you?' Jenny got in the passenger's side as Philips fired up the motor.

'It's a scrapes course.' Jenny wondered a moment if she need bother asking or not. 'I'll show you as we go past, but basically it's a dirt course, where you rake out the fairway kinda like a Japanese garden or bocce field and play golf instead.'

Jenny couldn't think of anything worse than walking around on dry dirt on a stinking hot day in Cobber Pedy hitting a ball around a field for eighteen holes. She'd never warmed to the game on grass, why on earth would she on sweltering, arid, sun-exposed dirt?

'We have a play off between the S.E.S and our station coming up, maybe you can give it a go.' He smiled.

'I'm terrible at golf. No one wants me on their team.'

'It's just a social get together, more an excuse to have a few beers than any serious competition, although Len used to take it pretty seriously.'

'Well lucky Len isn't stationed here anymore.' The words slipped out before she could stop herself. Her opinion of her predecessor wasn't shared by Philips, who seemed to believe the sun shone out of his arse, but the pout on her partner's lips told her she needed to keep a tighter rein on her mouth.

'He's alright.' He tried to convince her.

'If you're a guy maybe.'

'He's all talk.'

Jenny wanted to change the subject. The timing of Len's visit seemed off and how long was he going to stay? It wasn't exactly the Gold Coast. Coober Pedy was novel, for tourists keen to try Noodling—she smiled at the idea of even knowing what that was now—but it wasn't anyone's idea of a relaxing holiday and even if Len was visiting to catch up with mates, surely a day or two would be more than enough before he'd head back to Perth?

'How long is Len staying?'

'He didn't say. I reckon he needs some time away from the Missus, if you get my drift?' Philips pulled the police Landcruiser up to a mound of white and sulphur colour dirt and stopped. 'We're here.' They opened the doors in unison to the sound of loud arguing. Jenny was surprised to hear one of the voices sounded female.

'You flogged my jelly didn't you?'

'Mavis, give it a rest, you old chook.'

'Don't you brush me off Al. I know you took it.'

Having no idea what to expect when two miners didn't see eye to eye, Jenny followed Philips' lead.

'Mrs Carson. What's up?' He spoke casually, but Jenny could see by his stance he was alert. He needed to be. Mrs Carson was waving a double-barrel shotgun in Al's direction – *whoever Al was.*

Jenny resisted the urge to unclip her weapon. Instead she held back, giving herself plenty of room to manoeuvre or draw her gun or Taser if she needed it.

'Don't you Mrs Carson me Danny. I watched your mum change your nappies. You got no right interfering with my business.' She pointed the gun between Al and Philips as she spoke, her agitation obvious.

'She says I took her explosives but it wasn't me. I don't need 'em. I'm finished blasting for at least six months. It's all machinery from here out.' Al protested, his arms crossed, his legs splayed like he was having a casual talk with his mates. The fact that Mrs Carson was still waving her gun didn't seem to bother him at all.

'You know you can't be waving that thing around like that Mrs Carson!' Philips approached, gently pushing the barrel down toward the ground. Jenny's heart was in her mouth, the vein on her neck pulsed with adrenalin. How on earth was Philips being so calm?

'Shit Danny, you know I never keep it loaded.'

Philips grinned and took the gun from her hands, cracking the barrel and checking for good measure. Jenny was relieved to see he was at least following procedure. She told herself she needed to get to know the locals better.

'Someone stole my jelly.'

'How much?' Philips took a pen and paper out of his pocket and began to make some notes.

'Half a bloody kilo.'

Philips whistled. 'See anything Al? Any strange vehicles around?'

'Nah mate. Mavis probably forgot she used it.' He joked but it was obvious Mrs Carson didn't find him funny.

'Nothing wrong with my memory son.' She waved her finger in lieu of her gun.

'Show me where you keep it Mrs Carson.'

The woman's already lined face crinkled deeply before she turned and begun to walk away. Jenny noticed a severe limp as she waddled toward the entrance of her Dugout. The tin shed that designated the front of her home was rusty, with a recycled casement window hanging open at the front. A weathered wooden gate, complete with twisted wrought-iron handle, marked the front doorway.

She disappeared inside and Philips followed, holding the door open for Jenny to join him. 'Don't go anywhere just yet Al. I might need to talk to you still.'

The tall man wore a scraggly beard. His bald head was covered by a baseball cap that had seen better days and the flannelette shirt he wore over his trucker tank top had lost all the buttons.

'You got it Danny.' Al saluted as Jenny followed Philips inside, wondering how long it would take her eyes to adjust to the dimness, but she welcomed the coolness the overhanging rock offered.

Mrs Carson loomed over a worn leather chest, her arms crossed, her foot tapping impatiently. 'When you're ready son.'

'You kept it in here?' Philips turned his head sideways as he studied the box. Two leather straps usually buckled it shut—both were cut. A heavy gauge galvanised chain sat on the floor, the lock still intact. 'Where is the *Explosives* sign and the fire extinguisher?'

'Don't give me that rubbish. It was under lock and key. What more do you want?'

Philips didn't bother pointing out that there were numerous other guidelines relating to the storage of explosives that Mrs Carson failed to comply with and how non-compliance could cost her the explosives licence.

'See, it's been broken into.'

There was no point explaining that the lock and chain were rendered useless by the construction of the chest and the leather strapping used to secure it.

'What made you think it was Al?'

'Who else would it be? He's always getting by on the seat of his pants.'

'Who else knew you stored it here? In that chest?'

Mrs Carson thought a moment. 'I don't know, but it doesn't matter, we all store our jelly close to home, not like those fancy mining companies with their security guards and locked bunkers.' She rubbed her chin. Jenny noticed the fine grey hairs on her menopausal moustache collected dust from the mine, making it seem darker and more masculine. 'I guess anyone could have broken in and taken it.'

'When did you notice that it was missing?'

133

'This morning. I noticed the straps like that and the jelly was all gone.'

'So, during the night, someone broke in?' Philips continued to make notes.

'That's what I said son.'

'And you didn't wake up?' Mrs Carson stopped a moment, rubbed her hand over her top lip, removing some of the dirt.

'I'm not going senile Danny, but my hearing isn't what it used to be.' Jenny couldn't help thinking that blasting holes in the rock might not be so good for her hearing either, but she remained silent.

'We'll file the report but I'm not sure we are likely to find your explosives Mrs Carson.'

'Sure you will, just search Al's place or his ute.'

'We can't just do that Mrs Carson. Besides, one lot of explosives is hard to pick from another, unless of course you kept a record of the serial numbers?'

Mrs Carson scoffed.

'I'd suggest you consider a more secure way to store the explosives and you best make sure you include the signage and extinguisher Mrs Carson or I might have to report it to the licensing office.'

'Don't even think about it Danny. This is my livelihood you're messing with.' She shook her finger at him.

'It's your life I'm more interested in Mrs Carson and the lives of your neighbours. If the stolen explosives were taken by kids or someone wanting to do some real harm like a terrorist or something, people could get seriously hurt.'

Mrs Carson took a sharp breath, and frowned considering the warning. She nodded and Philips finished with his notes, placing the pad and pen in the front pocket of his utility vest. 'Now, be safe Mrs Carson and I'll let you know if anything comes of the report, but leave Al alone. Okay?'

Her nostrils flared, before she nodded a reluctant agreeance.

'Does that happen often?' Jenny asked as they returned to the vehicle.

'Miners arguing at gun point? Or the explosives being stolen?'

'Both.'

'Thanks Al, looks all good for now, but I'd give Mrs Carson a wide-birth for a few days.' Philips waved as they got in the four-wheel drive.

'No problem there Danny, thanks for coming out.' The miner returned the wave and set out across the red dirt toward a similar opening to Mrs Carson's, hidden behind recycled building materials in another hill of sandstone.

Philips started the car and pulled away down the dirt road that would take them back to the main highway.

'Mrs Carson is always pulling out that shotgun, but it's never loaded. Neighbour disputes aren't that common though. Claims are filed with the SA Energy and Mining office and they are clearly mapped out, so there isn't much motivation for claim jumping or trouble making. Still, tempers get a little frayed when the mine has been barren for a while.'

'And the explosives being stolen?'

'Now that is *un*common and a genuine cause for concern.'

Chapter 23

'Jenny, where are you? Can you talk?' The tension in Penny's voice made Jenny look around carefully as memories of last night's shadow filled her mind. She pulled her key from her pocket and opened her door.

'Sure. I'm just on my way to my room. What's up?'

'I've convinced my boss that I need another trip out to you so I can do a more thorough search of the mine where Tiffany's body was found.'

'Why?' Jenny closed her door and threw herself on the bed, the day's dust and sweat forgotten.

'Well, we found that fabric but we only searched around the body and that mine went in deeper. If we have a homicide—and I've probably convinced my boss we do—then we need to sift through the whole place and the surrounding area. I'll be down Sunday late afternoon ready to start work early Monday.'

'Does Sarge know?'

'He will Monday morning. Doc Holbrook sent a notice through email, but after mid-day today, so probably won't be seen until Monday first thing. But I didn't see any reason why we should wait. Evidence could be deteriorating.'

'Tiffany's been dead since June. Won't it all be long gone anyway?'

'DNA, yes, but this uniform fibre had traces of something on it that I'd like to investigate further. I want to see if I can find more pieces of cloth or something else that explains its presence. Maybe search Tiffany's personal belongings to see if I can find a match.'

'That's going to be tricky. I've tried to find where Tiffany was staying, and with whom, but no one seems to know. I think I need to pay Cheryl, her friend, another visit. I think she's keeping something from me but I don't understand why.'

'Sounds like a plan. Can you grab me from the airport Sunday, just after five p.m.?'

'Yep, I'll need to borrow someone's wheels, but I might ask Marj. I'm hoping to make a trip out to William Creek Station, but haven't heard if I'll be welcome yet.'

'Why wouldn't you be welcome? Isn't it a tourist spot?'

'It's a long story. I'll explain it when you get here. It's related to that case I told you about.'

'Okay. You didn't share much, but I'm looking forward to the rest of the backstory. Let me know if I can dig up some forensics for you.'

'I will, but there's been no new evidence, so nothing will have crossed your desk, well I hope not.' The idea that Melanie and Aunt Carolyn were dead in someone's morgue, unidentified, haunted Jenny's thoughts. Maybe she could get some DNA for Penny to check?

'See you at the airport then, Sunday.'

'Be great to have another friendly face.'

'Coober Pedy not welcoming the tall, thin, pretty cop then?'

Jenny laughed. 'Not exactly. Long story, but I'll talk to you soon.'

'Sounds intriguing. See you Sunday.'

'See you Sunday.' Jenny hung up, staring at the ceiling of the motel a moment before remembering she was covered in dirt and smelt like a gym locker.

Fifteen minutes later, the flowery smell of her deodorant filled the air, lifting her spirits. Bundling her filthy uniforms from the past few days into a garbage bag, she added her underwear, a night shirt and a few items that needed cleaning and headed for the laundry. On the way, she called past Reception.

'Jenny, how are you?

'Good thanks Marj. It's been a crazy first week though.'

'I wondered why I hadn't seen you much.' The motel owner seemed even chirpier than usual, especially for a Saturday afternoon. Maybe the motel was full of tourists or there was a big restaurant booking for the weekend.

'Marj, I was wondering if I could hire a car from somewhere?' Jenny knew she probably could, but she was hopeful Marj would know where to scrounge one up at a good price.

'What do you need it for?'

'Two things. I'm hoping to head out to William Creek Station tomorrow and I need to pick up a friend from the airport late in the afternoon. It's kind of a work thing, but I don't have a work car, only Philips and O'Connell do.'

'You pay for the fuel and you can borrow my old Navara ute. She's not exactly flash, but she'll get you from A to B and the air conditioner still works.'

'What more can a girl ask for? That's very kind of you Marj.'

'No trouble at all, now don't you spend your evening washing clothes when you could be chatting up those nice young men in the bar now will you?'

'I'm sure there are plenty of other lovely local girls to keep them occupied.' Jenny changed her garbage bag from one hand to the other.

'Oh come on now Constable Williams, you have raised the bar a little for the local girls now haven't you?'

Jenny's eyebrows rose. What did that even mean? She was tall, lanky, socially awkward and didn't own a curling iron, hairspray or even a bottle of nail polish.

As if sensing Jenny's confusion, Marj leant over the reception counter and wiggled her finger for her to come closer. When she did, Marj whispered. 'You are the prettiest girl in town Jenny. All the young men are lining up to ask you out, but being a police officer, well that's slowing them down a little.'

Jenny grinned, thinking of how it hadn't slowed Nev one little bit, but maybe her position as a police officer was why Nick was so aloof. But that would have only made sense if he were romantically interested in her and he'd shown no signs he was. Maybe just being a cop was enough to put him on edge. The thought made her wonder if he'd told her the truth about her family.

'I don't think they are that intimidated Marj. I've fended off a few offers, but I'm here to work, not to play.' She hugged her washing to her chest.

'You have to let your hair down sometimes Jenny. Life is too short not to.' Marj collected a set of keys from the back wall of the office and threw them to jenny who caught them deftly. 'She's my spare, so keep her as long as you need, but you break her, you bought her, okay?'

'I'll look after the car Marj.'

'Red.' Jenny stopped with one foot out the door and turned.

'Red?'

'I call her Red.'

'The car?'

'Yes, she's more burgundy than red, but she makes me think of red wine, so Red.'

'You named your car?'

'Sure, doesn't everyone?' Marj chuckled and Jenny shook her head, put the keys in her pocket and left to finish her washing.

She entered the motel laundry. Finding it empty, she put her washing into the closest washing machine, used a few coins to dispense some powder—reminding herself to go shopping for a more environmentally friendly washing liquid—then set the machine going.

She pulled out her mobile and checked her personal email account. Nick's reply was cryptic. Was it a yes, or a no?

Don't think they'll know anything, but knock yourself out if you have to.

'Well Mr Johnston, don't mind if I do,' she said aloud, before putting her phone in her pocket and leaving her washing to finish while she headed to the bar for a drink and a catch up with Tim and Nev. Hopefully Cheryl would be on the bar tonight and she'd be able to find out what the woman wasn't telling her about where Tiffany was staying before she went missing.

Chapter 24

Jenny spotted Nev waving as she entered the bar. He sat with Tim and a few of their work colleagues, while Philips sat two tables over with his wife Dianna and their son Tommy. The boy was hoeing into a plate of chicken nuggets and chips like there was no tomorrow. Dianna smiled. Jenny waved a quick hello.

Cheryl was serving at the bar, so she stopped at Nev's table a moment. 'You guys want a drink?'

'No, my shout.' Nev got up, his hand already dipping into this back pocket for his wallet.

'It's fine. Let me buy you at least one drink before my first week is up. Besides, I need to talk to Cheryl.'

Nev glanced at the barmaid, then back to Jenny, nodding his understanding. 'Okay, but I'm doing the next round.' Tim and Nev were already nursing a beer, making her decision on what to order easy.

'Hi Cheryl. Can I get a jug of Coopers ale thanks.' Jenny pulled her credit card from her back pocket as Cheryl poured the jug and put it on top of the bar, the frothy head spilling over slightly onto the bar mat.

'Will that be all?' she asked, her voice in work mode, devoid of any real emotion.

'You okay Cheryl?' The woman nodded. 'I need to ask you a few more questions about Tiffany, where she was living, who else might have been staying with her. That kind of thing. Can I catch you a bit later maybe?'

'I'm busy until after eleven and I've already told you all I know.'

'I don't think you have.' Cheryl lifted the EFTPOS machine to the counter and Jenny tapped her card to pay. She watched as the woman's eyes lifted from the machine and focussed on something over Jenny's shoulder, her eyes diverted so quickly, it gave Jenny tingles.

Turning around she found the source of Cheryl's discomfort walking over to join Philips and his wife. It seemed Len Holmes didn't give just her the creeps.

'You know him?' Jenny asked as she put her card back in her pocket, her eyes following Len who was staring at her talking with Cheryl rather than Philips, as he took a seat next to Dianna.

'Everyone knows Officer Len Holmes.' The words were carefully measured and spaced out like they were more than an official police title.

'You don't like him?'

Cheryl shrugged too casually and Jenny knew now wasn't the time to push. 'Can I see you when you finish at eleven? I know it's late, but I'd rather a casual talk here, than have to bring you down the station on Monday.' Cheryl's eyebrows lifted. Jenny was bluffing. She wasn't likely to bring Cheryl in for official questioning when she was supposed to be running a quiet investigation, but the threat did the trick.

'Where do you want to meet?'

'You can come to my room, number twelve.' Cheryl nodded.

Jenny picked up the jug and two chilled glasses. She dodged a seven or so year old boy, towing his little sister at warp speed toward the play room before weaving her way back to Nev and friends, via Philips' table in the hopes of catching even a hint of Len's conversation. All she heard was a brief few words about when Tommy was starting day-care.

'Took you long enough.' Nev held up his empty glass and Jenny chuckled.

'There's a band playing tonight. You hanging around?' Tim asked as he held his glass out for a top up. Jenny obliged before filling her own.

'Anyone else need a glass?' She placed the spare on the table next to the jug of beer that was already half empty. 'I don't know Tim. It's been one hell of a week.'

'That's for sure.' Nev took a swig of beer. 'Any update on Tiffany's death?'

'At this stage, it's being ruled death by misadventure.'

'But?' Nev leant forward conspiratorially.

'But nothing. The boss has called it. I've been told to pull my head in, so case closed.' Jenny spoke loud enough that if Philips was listening in, he'd have heard.

'Sure it is.' Tim chuckled. 'So what are you doing with all those volunteer lists I emailed you?'

Jenny felt eyes on her back, suddenly wishing she'd sat facing Philips and his family.

'I requested those before the boss chewed me out for being overzealous. They'll get filed with the final reports.' She could only hope Philips would believe she wasn't pursuing the case and that Tim would be satisfied to let the matter go.

'You didn't give a definitive answer to the question Constable Williams.' Tim's tone was half teasing. Jenny's entire body was winding up like a spring ready to release. She needed to get him to change the subject. 'Are you staying for a few more beers and a few tunes?'

She laughed and relaxed. 'Maybe. But I need to do my washing.'

'Shit Jenny, that's worse than *I need to wash my hair* when it comes to lame excuses why you shouldn't be out partying.' Nev nudged her in the ribs with his beer still in hand, fortunately he'd already nearly drained the glass and nothing spilled over.

'You drink like a fish Nev.' He answered her comment with a smile.

'Avoiding answering the question. Great evasive techniques. She's good.' He nodded toward Tim who raised his glass in salute.

Marj's voice sounded in her head. She had to agree, it was a lame excuse. 'Okay, you win. I'll eat dinner, then switch my washing over to the dryer and join you, for a while. Satisfied?'

Both guys grinned mischievously, making her glad of their persistence. Coober Pedy was going to be a real lonely place if she didn't get her head out of her arse and find some friends. At least these guys were shaping up to be alright. She hoped once this Tiffany case was over with, Cheryl might be a great person to get to know better too. No doubt the girl could do with a few decent friends. The last thing she wanted was to see another Tiffany case in town because no one took the time to genuinely care.

****

Jenny watched Philips pick up a sleeping Tommy from his wife's lap. The blonde-haired boy looked so peaceful with his arms hanging loosely over Danny's shoulder.

'My Uncle lives out near William Creek Station. He reckons the place is cursed.' Nev was chatting fluidly now, well into his fifth beer for the evening.

Jenny drew her attention away from her co-worker as he escorted his wife from the motel bar and restaurant. The band was just getting ready to play, tuning instruments and checking the sound system as she watched Len leave with Philips. She couldn't help wondering why the guy was hanging out with Danny, who was probably twenty years his junior.

'Why does your Uncle live so far out in the middle of nowhere?' Jenny focussed on Nev, who was trying to focus on his beer. Tim was at the bar looking to refill their beer jug and Jenny thought that might not be wise, but shrugged the idea away. It was Saturday night after all and there wasn't much else for these guys to do to keep them occupied.

'He's a local Elder. Won't have a bar of city life.' Nev laughed and Jenny grinned at the idea that Coober Pedy ranked in anyone's mind as a city. 'He moves around a bit, sometimes he's out at the Umoona Community, other times, he's tracking and working as a Jackaroo. He used to work at William Creek, but he quit a while back.'

Jenny's interest was piqued. 'Did he work there nine or ten years ago?'

'I'm not sure. Maybe. I was away finishing up at university around that time, or maybe even interning in Adelaide. Why?'

'Just curious.' She didn't want to share too much just yet, but Nev's uncle might be worth chatting to, especially if Nick's workers weren't of any use. 'I guessed you had indigenous genes when I first met you, but didn't realise you came from around here. I should have realised.'

'My mum is Ngurabanna, like my uncle and my dad was a white fella.' Nev allowed his accent to return as he used the word 'fella', Jenny found it cute, but wondered why he usually kept it hidden. 'The land, it draws us back.'

'I thought that might be like an old wives' tale.'

'No. It isn't. I loved the city life and university, but it got old quick. There is something spiritual about this place. I'll take you out to the homelands sometime, show you what I mean. You can meet the mob, my family.'

'That would be awesome Nev. I know next to nothing about aboriginal heritage. Just the political stuff, like *Sorry Day* and what they taught us in school—which wasn't much.

'It's a tough subject. White fellas didn't know any better back then.'

'But they do now.' Jenny assured him.

'Some, yeah. Some, not so much.'

Jenny watched Nev down his beer as Tim returned with a top up. She could sense he was a little melancholy after speaking of his heritage. Walking the line between worlds must be difficult, but she didn't know him well enough to pry.

'I need to go switch my washing to the dryer. I'll be back in ten.' They acknowledged her with a wave as the band started playing *Livin' on a Prayer,* highlighting the age demographic of the room.

Despite the old hit her parents listened to, Jenny found herself humming the tune on her way to the laundry.

She opened the washing machine, her vision swam a little, warning her she might have already drunk too much. Loading the dryer, she closed the door and pressed start, deciding to slow things down a little or she'd be in no state to get up early and head out to Nick's place. These country boys certainly knew how to pack the grog away.

She took a shortcut, bypassing the well-lit walkway for a quick walk across the artificial turf that lined the courtyard. The area was bordered by thick, healthy and flowering grevillea bushes, which gave an almost honeysuckle sent to the warm night air.

Her senses reeled as a hand grabbed her by the mouth and dragged her further into the shadows. Jenny's reactions were slow as she kicked her assailant in the shin and turned her head, just like she'd been trained, to release his hold on her mouth, but he was ready.

As his grip tightened, he held her to him. His chest heaved at her back, the smell of beer wafted into her nostrils as he whispered. 'Get your nose out of it before someone else gets hurt.'

Jenny struggled, but he was too strong, his arm held one hand to her side in a bear hug, the other hand was free, but she couldn't get a hold of anything, even his hair was too short to grasp.

'Hey. What's going on?' someone called from the car park.

Jenny's attacker shoved her hard into the bushes. She stumbled, recovering just enough of her balance to land lightly, headfirst into the coarse foliage.

Adrenalin fired and she turned to see the assailant moving toward the far end of the courtyard, where the commercial rubbish bins and service carpark were. Without a second thought, she took chase, Philips close behind.

Neither of them spoke as they searched the darkness without any luck. A few moments passed without a sound as Jenny peered into the night, the only light behind the motel came from the quarter moon and the canopy of stars above.

'He's gone.' Philips offered. 'Are you okay? Did he hurt you?'

'Just my pride.' Jenny turned back toward the restaurant, suddenly alert with a craving for something stronger than beer to settle her nerves.

'What did he want? Did he steal anything?'

Jenny wondered what she should say. She wasn't supposed to be on Tiffany's case, or maybe this was related to her cousin and aunt? Either way, she decided to be vague or Philips would know she was still hunting down a possible killer.

'He just told me to stop being nosey.'

'Nosey about what?' Philips opened the restaurant door and stopped with a gentle hand on her arm. 'You sure you want

147

to go back in?' The sound of the band music playing another hit from the nineties made her even more determined not to let this guy put her off. She knew now she was definitely on to something, the only issue was, she was yet to figure out what.

'I'm okay Danny.' She used his first name, hoping it would make it all less official. 'I appreciate the help though. You made him run, which was a good thing.'

'He looked familiar.'

Jenny stopped in the open doorway, music blaring out into the night. She hadn't seen her assailant clearly, only his back as he disappeared behind the motel. 'Really? Who do you think it was?'

Philips went to speak but thought better of it and shrugged. 'I'm not sure. If I think of who, I'll let you know.'

Chapter 25

Jenny was up before the sun, desperate to get on the road before it got too hot. She'd waited up an extra hour, hoping Cheryl was just running late, but by midnight it became clear she was not going to show. The lack of sleep was going to make driving most of the day hard, but the excitement of finally getting somewhere with her family's case kept her motivated.

William Creek Station was over two hours away and she wanted as much time as possible to be able to talk to all the people who worked with Nick Johnston and may have met her aunt or cousin.

She placed the photos she kept of them in her backpack, added a bottle of water, her phone, a few protein bars and her hat. With her belongings still in transit, the only sun protection available was her work Akubra. It would have to do.

The Australian desert was no place to mess around and a single woman, travelling in an older, less reliable vehicle needed to be prepared. If her car broke down, she could die of thirst or exposure before she was rescued, especially considering how dubious the phone reception was that far out of Coober Pedy.

To keep her occupied as she drove, she loaded her smartphone with a playlist of her favourite songs from when she and Melanie used to hang out together. Justin Timberlake singing *Sexy Back* sent her memory tumbling back to their final year of school. The boys, the beach days, the football games and farm adventures they shared. Then she'd gone away for a Mother-Daughter holiday—a celebration of her entry to university, living away from home in Adelaide. Now she was gone.

Mel was smart, super intelligent in fact. She used to win all the maths competitions and took out class honours in their final year together. If Mel had started at university, she would have been one of the youngest ever at barely seventeen.

'I'll find you Mel, one way or another. I'll find you.' She made the promise as Nickelback sang *Photograph* on her phone, and the sun rose slowly, greeting a new day, highlighting the vast open desert which offered her no comfort. She fought to keep her teary eyes on the road and her mind on the here and now.

****

Two hours later, Jenny's butt was numb and her neck stiff and sore as she drove the old four-wheel drive under the tall gate sign with faded letters, written in what was once dark green and terracotta colours. *William Creek Station* – the sign, written back when sign writers did everything by hand, not with computer graphics or plotted vinyl lettering – announced her arrival.

The long, dirt road took a straight line, like a runway all the way to a homestead that sat in the distance like a mirage. Greyish saltbush and native grasses dotted the landscape as small herds of cattle roamed around bales of hay locked behind round metal cages that prevented the animals from eating it all at once.

Occasional black poly drinking troughs appeared along the roadside, where small clusters of cattle gathered. The absence of shade was mind blowing and Jenny couldn't help but wonder how the animals survived such inhospitable surroundings, but she knew they did. In fact, they thrived out here, in some of the largest cattle-station land in the country.

Where she came from the grass was two feet high, dark green from nitrogen rich soils, with rows of tall gum trees protecting the cattle from the harsh sun. Out here, it was the land of drought or flooding rains.

As the homestead drew closer, Jenny realised it was a cluster of buildings, with a gradual hillside rising behind them. A perimeter of hardy native shrubs created a windbreak that offered a greyish, greenish hedge to break up the stark red, white, ochre and yellow earth that surrounded the area.

The dust cloud that followed her along the road, no doubt alerted the homestead to her arrival. As she drove through the treed boundary, she passed the shearing shed, cattle yards and a series of workers' quarters.

Two jackaroos sat on the front porch step of their accommodation. The first had a rolled cigarette perched on his lip, barely noticeable against his greying beard. The second was likely half his age, but bore the same rugged dark, weather-worn face that said he'd seen years of hard work on the land.

The latter tipped his hat as she waved and drove slowly by. Drawing the vehicle up outside the main homestead, Jenny couldn't help but admire the long, covered veranda, complete with two wooden lounges framing the double door entrance.

Two men and a woman waited on the sandstone pavers, watching her intently as she turned off the engine and got out. Sam smiled when he recognised her. The woman plonked her hands on her hips, turning to Nick, who stared at Jenny with wide eyes. He'd learn to understand she didn't give up easily.

'Constable Williams.' Sam jumped down from the veranda and shook her hand. What are you doing all the way out here?'

'Your brother didn't tell you I was coming?' Jenny looked past Sam. Her eyes fell on Nick, who didn't move a muscle. The woman beside him glanced from her to Nick, her brow creased, her lips curled into a suppressed snarl.

'No. Is this about the accident?'

'No Sam. I'm confident you're all clear on that front. I told you I'd put in a good word for you.'

Sam grinned. 'Thanks for that. I appreciate it. Old man Mackenzie can be a real arse at times.'

'Tell me about it.' She rolled her eyes and Sam laughed. 'But I'm not on duty today, so let's not talk about Sergeant Mackenzie.' Jenny watched Nick as she spoke.

'Let me introduce you.' Sam ushered her onto the veranda, his friendly nature and big smile such a massive contrast from his brother. 'You've met my brother Nick. This is Rebecca.'

'Pleased to meet you Rebecca. I'm Jenny.' The woman took the offered hand reluctantly. 'I'm sorry to disturb your Sunday, but Nick said I could come out and ask a few questions about a cold case I'm working on.'

Rebecca glared at Nick who hadn't said a word, or taken his eyes from Jenny but his expression softened.

'Nick?' Rebecca turned on him.

'Jenny, Constable Williams has…'

'A cold case.' Jenny prompted and Nick raised an eyebrow, realising she didn't want to reveal her relationship to Melanie and Carolyn just yet.

'Missing persons case.' Nick continued. 'It was while I was away, at Uni. I checked the records and Dad's books showed they never arrived, but Constable…'

'Please call me Jenny. This isn't an official investigation. I'm just chalking up brownie points.' She decided brown nosing would be her cover for this enquiry. Nothing official, just trying to impress the boss.

Rebecca rolled her eyes as Nick continued. 'Jenny just wants to ask the workers who were probably here at the time, what they might know.'

'And when were you going to tell me about this?'

'It's my fault.' Jenny interrupted. 'I don't think Nick realised I meant I'd be out *this* weekend. I should have called ahead.'

'Now I guess you want me to go and print off a list of who worked here?' She huffed and Jenny nodded. 'When?'

'I didn't mean to be a pain.'

'You're not.' Nick turned stiffly toward the woman. 'Rebecca is paid to do the admin on the property. *Aren't you?*' Her hazel eyes regarded him with controlled hostility.

'When?' she asked again.

'Between September twentieth, to October ninth, two thousand and six.' The woman flicked her long, straight dark brown pony tail as she spun round to head into the homestead.

'How about a cold drink?' Sam offered, directing Jenny through the entrance. A spacious hallway opened to a wide staircase with a cased opening either side leading into the main living areas of the building. Below the stairs, Jenny could see a passageway leading to the left and beyond, the hallway continued with more doors leading from it.

'This place is gorgeous. When was it built? I saw an old homestead on the drive in, sandstone, but derelict now.'

'That's the original homestead, built nearly two hundred years ago by our relatives.' Sam seemed proud of the family history, but as usual, Nick was quiet just following along behind her, keeping his distance.

There was obviously some tension between him and Rebecca but was it business or personal? She told herself it was none of her business. She needed to stay focused on finding out about her cousin.

'This homestead was built in the late twenties, by our Grandad.' Sam continued.

Jenny admired the federation fretwork that hung below the balcony to the second floor. The wooden floors were jarrah or redgum and shone from years of polishing and wear.

'The kitchen is up the back here.' Jenny followed Sam, still acutely aware that Nick had said nothing more. As they reached the kitchen, she turned to wait for him.

'I'm sorry I didn't confirm. I should have.' Sam moved past the large, casual dining table to the fridge and pulled out a jug of orange juice.

'Juice okay?'

'Thanks.' Jenny nodded without taking her eyes from Nick's. 'I'm also sorry I didn't want anyone to know this is personal for me.' She whispered the latter.

Nick nodded, but still said nothing. What was up with him? 'Here you go.' Sam handed Jenny and Nick a drink, before taking a seat at the colonial dining table. Jenny finally took in the entire room, which must have been an addition. It was wide, and open, with floor to ceiling windows that embraced the escarpment beyond.

The rusty red hills rose into the distance, and further on she could just make out strange mountains. They reminded her of giant stalagmites rising through eroded hillsides.

She sucked in a quick breath and took a moment to absorb the view. 'Magnificent. They remind me of the Glasshouse Mountains in Queensland.'

'What I'd give for their rainfall.' Jenny turned to Nick, who took a sip of his drink before pulling his chair out to sit. 'This place is magical, but farming here is tough.'

'I can only imagine, but if you received Queensland's rainfall – hell if you even got the rainfall we get back at my home farm – you'd be under water.'

Nick smiled for the first time and Jenny's breath hitched. His blue eyes twinkled, and deep lines on his forehead were replaced with tiny smile lines that were too immature for a man his age.

The creaking of floorboards told them they had company. Nick's smile disappeared. Jenny's stomach knotted as his face became grim once more.

'Done. Anything else before I head off?' Rebecca's tone said there better not be, but Nick didn't seem to notice.

'That's it. See you Monday,' Rebecca huffed, turned and stomped hard enough to make the homestead echo in her wake.

Jenny questioned Nick with her eyes, but he only shrugged. He wasn't in a hurry to elaborate on the cause of Rebecca's foul mood. Someone in town would have the gossip, she was sure of it. Maybe Mrs B. from the William Creek pub would offer insight. Sam and Mick were best friends after all.

Nick handed Jenny the list. Only five names were on it. 'Is this all the staff who worked here back then?'

'No. It's all we had then, and are still with us now.'

'Damn. I wanted all the staff, so I could chase them down here and wherever they are now.'

'I'll ask Rebecca to forward it to you Monday.'

Jenny read the names. *John Butler, Seth Goodard, Josh Thompson, Albert* and *Edward.* 'The last two don't have surnames.' Nick nodded.

'They are indigenous. Lived here all their lives. No need for last names in the community.'

'I think I saw them on the way in. Older guy with a grey beard and a younger guy, cheeky smile?'

'That's them. They are born horsemen, and Albert is a fine tracker, not that we need one very often but he reads the signs.' Jenny was pleased Nick was finally sharing something about his life. She found talking about work always loosened lips.

'Can we start with them then?'

'We could, but they just rode out to muster some cattle after you got here.'

'When will they be back?'

'A few days.'

'But I came out to speak with them.' Jenny knew she sounded defensive.

'This is a working station. We don't pay the bills sitting around eating cakes and drinking juice.'

'You're right, I'm sorry. Can we ride out with them?'

Sam glanced up from reading an old copy of the Stock Journal.

'I'll take her.'

'No. You stay here, man the phones and keep the cook on schedule.'

'But.'

'No buts Sam.' He turned to Jenny. 'You said you could ride, right?'

'Right.'

'This isn't a picnic. These cattle are wild and they wouldn't think twice about lifting you and your horse and sending you heavenward.'

'I get it. I've done camp drafting as a teenager.'

'Not the same.'

'I'll be careful. I'm not planning on herding any cattle. I just want to show the boys a picture and ask a few questions.'

He pushed up from the table. Jenny did the same. His eyes swept up and down her body. At first she thought he was assessing her ability from her looks. 'At least you're dressed for it.'

She chewed her lip. Was that a compliment? What did he expect, high heels and a cocktail dress?

Chapter 26

'What are these for?' Jenny asked as she swung her leg over the swag tied to her horse's rump—the polished leather stock saddle squeaking as she settled into the seat.

'It's a decent ride out. You never know out here either. If we get rain, we could get stuck out for a few days.'

'Hopefully not, I've got work tomorrow.' She thought about Penny needing a pick up from the airport. Maybe she should have allowed more time to come out here. 'Why not take a car then?'

'Because all the vehicles are being used except my four-wheel drive and that has to stay at the homestead in case of an emergency.'

'Oh.'

'You aren't working today, are you?'

'Not unless there is an emergency call out, but I guess I'll be out of range.' She smiled at the thought and what O'Connell and Sarge would have to say about that, but no one told her she needed to stay in town. Maybe she should have said where she was going though?

As they rode past a fenced area, she noticed a small graveyard. 'That the family plot?' Nick nodded. 'I heard about your dad. Sorry.'

'Why? It wasn't your fault.' Nick nudged his horse into a gentle canter and Jenny followed his lead. The move was obviously his way of preventing further conversation and Jenny saw no reason to force him to talk. It was none of her business.

They rode nearly two hours in the hot sun before they reached a low lying, dry river bed. Green grass sprouted from the sand like a caterpillar winding its way along a concrete driveway. Hundreds of cattle mowed it down by the mouthful and Jenny couldn't stop gawking.

'Where does the water come from?'

'Rain, we get nearly the whole annual rainfall in a few weeks here and it runs to the lowest point.' He pointed to the white and sandy coloured hills that Jenny recognised from the homestead windows. 'Plus, there are a few springs dotted around these areas. They feed the low land throughout the rest of the year.'

'It's beautiful.'

Nick watched her survey the landscape, the line of his lips softening into a gentle smile, but he lost it as soon as she looked back at him. *Why did he hate smiling so much?*

'Why build the homestead so far away from this spot then?'

'It's not the only riverbed, plus the homestead is close to the Oodnadatta Track, which is the main transportation route. The trucks have to pick the cattle up and take them to market, and out here is way too far from a pick-up point.'

Nick trotted his horse toward three horsemen who were spread out along the line of cattle, doing their best to get the herd to move away from the feed.

'Looks like we'll need the chopper,' he called to the first.

'For sure Boss. I've called Roger in. He's about fifteen minutes out.'

'Good. That should be long enough.'

'For what?'

'Jenny, this is Russ. Russ, Jenny is the new Constable in town and she's got a cold case that goes back to Albert and Ed's time. Just a few questions and we'll be out of your hair.'

'Go for it.' He waved them past and Jenny matched pace with Nick as they worked their way along the line of cattle that were passive enough with food keeping them occupied.

'Al, Ed. Got a sec?' Nick called as he rode up alongside.

'Sure.' Ed answered as they reined their horses in.

Jenny reached into her pocket and pulled out a photo of her aunt and cousin. 'Do you recognise either of these women? They would have visited the homestead for a trail ride tour back in late September two thousand six?'

Ed looked at the photo, but Jenny didn't hold out much hope. The guy was likely around her age, maybe a few years older and probably not that interested in the comings and goings of tourists.

'Yeah, remember her.' She quickly hid her surprise.

'And the other woman?'

'Nope. Dad?' He passed it to the older man, whose rolled-up smoke still hung from his lips. Jenny thought it might be the same one, since it had long since stopped burning, something common with *rollies,* but Albert didn't seem too bothered about it.

'Nope, but me eyes ain't what day used to be.'

'Where did you see the younger woman Edward? Any information you can give me would be great.'

'At the homestead. Only briefly, but she was definitely hard to forget when you're eighteen, all the girls catch your attention.' Jenny smiled. Melanie always turned heads. They bore similar features, but Melanie was shorter, curvier, more feminine than Jenny.

'Where at the homestead?' Nick leant forward in his saddle so he could hear over the buzzing sound that was growing louder. A crease formed over his brow as he waited for the answer.

'I was going to the cookhouse and she was with your dad.' He gazed down into his weathered hands then, a sadness fell across his face.

'What was she doing?' Nick pushed on, seemingly unconcerned over his father's death.

'I don't know, carrying a load of gear. She looked out of sorts, like she'd been throwing up or was sick.'

'Thanks Ed.' Nick turned to Jenny. 'We need to move. The chopper will have this herd moving in a hurry soon. Follow me.' He nudged his horse firmly and the animal lunged into a full canter, slowed slightly for the rocky edge of the dry riverbed, then pushed on. Jenny needed all her rusty skills to keep up, but as the helicopter drew closer and the cattle began to scatter, she knew falling off wasn't an option.

Nick led them up the hillside of the first strange, prehistoric looking mountain. It wasn't much more than a hill, but her horse slipped and skidded. Jenny tightened her grip on the reins. Her shoulders tensed. If her mount lost his footing now, it could kill them both.

'We'll watch from here.' Nick reined his horse around and Jenny followed suit. 'You ride okay for a townie.'

Jenny smiled. 'I told you I rode as a kid.'

'You did, but I've hosted our trail rides and I hear that all the time. Dressage girls who can trot their mounts around a sandy arena, but fall arse over as soon as they hit rough terrain.'

'I grew up on a dairy farm.'

'You said a farm before. Dairying hey. Whereabouts?'

'Myponga, south of Adelaide.'

'Never been there.'

'Adelaide?' She teased and he grinned. Those eyes again.

'Adelaide I've been to. That's where I did my degree, but Myponga, never been there.'

'It's quiet, cold in winter, warm in summer, not as warm as here, but hot enough. Green, hilly, mostly dairy country although these days it's full of hobby farmers who want big houses on acreage near the city.'

They watched the chopper fly over as cattle began to scramble. 'That got them moving.' Jenny grinned, remembering how she used to herd the cows back home with the four-wheeled motorbike.

'Usually does.'

'What do you make of Edward's information?' She knew it must be difficult talking about his dad, especially now that he might have made a mistake with his booking information. 'Are you sure your dad kept good records?'

'Ed could be mistaken. One pretty girl could be confused with another.' He held her gaze, then focused on his reins.

'I wish I could confirm it with bank records, but credit card receipts going back nearly ten years ago require a court ordered warrant and I don't have enough evidence to get that— not while they are missing.' She left the rest unsaid, but Nick seemed to read between the lines.

Until bodies were found, her relatives could still be alive and warrants to search private records would never be approved.

'Does anyone know you're looking into your cousin's disappearance? Other than me?'

'O'Connell, Penny.'

'Penny?'

'A friend.' Well she was becoming a friend. 'Forensic scientist from the Adelaide crime lab.'

Nick nodded. 'We better head back if you have work on Monday.'

'We aren't following the mob?'

'No. I thought you might like to see the escarpment. We've got indigenous art on the property. I'll show you on the way back.' Nick nudged his mount forward and Jenny considered how sensible it was to stay out here, alone with a stranger, one who employed all the witnesses who knew Melanie visited the Station, even though Nick's dad never recorded her arrival.

Chapter 27

A chill ran down Jenny's back as she stared up at the rock formation. She'd never seen anything like it—white, ochre, brown figures painted like tiny skeletons on the walls, telling a story of aboriginal history going back thousands of years.

'This is amazing. How old are these?'

'Some, like this one,' he pointed to a white faced skeleton man standing with a group of brown skeleton figures, spears in hand. 'date back to early white settlers.'

'Your relatives then?' She pointed to the lonely white figure.

'Possibly. I'd have to ask the elders, but most likely.'

'And these ones, of the animals?'

'Some are Dreamtime stories, handed down through the generations. This is like an encyclopaedia to the aboriginal people. This one is a celebration of an initiation ceremony. This place is sacred for the ritual.'

'Do you let the tribes use the land here still to celebrate their rituals?'

'Of course. Like the indigenous people of this land, we are just caretakers, only we raise cattle here. The local tribes come and go through these lands as they please. They can hunt and kill any native animals, gather whatever berries they want, but many young men don't participate in the initiation anymore.'

Jenny thought of Nev who left to study and become a doctor. He'd returned to the area. A child of both worlds.

'We better get you back.'

Jenny scanned her watch. 'Damn. I wish I could stay but I have to pick Penny up from the airport.'

Nick ducked out of the cave. Jenny followed after a lingering backward glance. A short walk back to the horses found them standing obediently, their ears alert as their riders approached. 'I have to admit, I didn't expect you to be so accommodating.'

'Really?' He collected his reins from the bush he'd flung them over, grabbed the pommel and vaulted into the saddle.

'When I met you at the hospital, you didn't exactly look happy to meet the new cop in town.' Jenny put her foot in the stirrup and swung up, settling into the saddle.

Nick said nothing, just nudged his horse down the narrow trail that led them from the escarpment down to the wide open, sun-drenched land below.

'Do you get lonely out here?' Nick waited for her to draw her horse alongside, the smell of his aftershave drifted on the warm breeze. The scent of nutmeg and sandalwood, mixed with leather filled her senses.

'Not often. Sam likes to be around people, but I find it hard to trust people so I prefer my own company, for the most part.'

'You don't trust the police, do you?' Nick shrugged.

'Did you want a muesli bar?' He pulled two packets from his saddle bag, ignoring her comment. 'It's not exactly a feast, but it should keep us going til we get back. The cook should have something sorted.'

'You didn't answer my question.' Jenny took the bar and tore it open before taking a small bite.

'When my father died, it was ruled suicide. By the time I got back from university, his body was already released for burial and the case was closed.' Jenny watched him closely. 'Sam was too young to fully understand what was going on.'

'You don't think it was suicide?'

'It wasn't, but the alternative is that my mum killed him before she disappeared and I don't like that idea any better.'

'Oh Nick. I'm sorry.' She wanted to reach over and touch him, but didn't. 'It looks like the local police missed a few cases that crossed their desk. My cousin and aunt, and maybe your dad's death.' Nick nodded. 'Do you remember who was in charge then?'

'Sergeant Mackenzie has been in Coober Pedy since I was in primary school. Len nearly as long, but it was Len Holmes who met me and went over the reports. When I pushed him to open the investigation again, he patted my arm and told me to go home, look after my brother and let it go.'

'Just like that.'

'Yeah. Just like that.'

'Did you let it go?'

'Never.'

Jenny finished her bar and put the wrapper in her pocket. 'That's how I feel about Melanie and Aunt Carolyn.'

'I'll do what I can to help, but I don't know what I can do. Dad didn't record them staying, so it doesn't make a lot of sense that Ed saw Melanie here.'

'Mrs B. at the pub said they skipped out without paying their bill, but that isn't like them. Something strange is going on Nick and I need to dig around and find out, but I'm tied up with another case right now. I appreciate your help though.'

'What case?'

'Tiffany Cox's death.' She wondered why she was telling him any of this. He had been so cool with her until today. As she gazed out over the landscape, she knew she was letting her barriers fall away for the first time in nearly a decade. 'You think it's murder?'

'Let's say it's suspicious.' She unscrewed the top from her water canteen and took a long sip, the water still cool in the insulated container. 'Did you go to the Opal Festival last June?'

'No. We were hosting visitors that week, in the homestead. It's a huge place, lots of rooms and most of them are empty. We used to host families for trail rides, like we did when your relatives planned to stay, but now we usually have wealthier clients. During the festival, they fly by chopper to Coober Pedy each day. Or take a light plane. Our lives are like a game to them.'

'Why host them then?' Nick smiled across at her, his eyes attractive, yet haunted.

'I would have lost this place years ago if we hadn't changed our business plan. Cattle make plenty of money when we have feed, but until recently, we'd seen years of drought.'

'Rebecca helped with the plans? Is she an employee, family?' She wasn't sure why she needed to ask the question, but she couldn't help but wonder why the woman was so aggressive when they met.

'Rebecca is like a sister. I've known her for years. We grew up together and our parents thought we'd get married, take over the station and pub together, but that was never going to happen.'

'The pub?'

'Rebecca's family own the pub.'

'She's Mick's sister?'

'Yeah. Great family, hard-working, but Rebecca has worked for the Station for years. Mrs B. still runs the pub, but Mick will take over after he finishes university. Unless he doesn't.'

'What's Sam going to be studying?'

'He's taking another gap year, to work on the property, travel a bit. I'm not sure what he'll study.'

'Did you finish your degree?'

'Not at first. I came home to run the property. We have over fifteen thousand head here. It's been a good year, but some years we have so little rain, that our carrying capacity drops to less than ten thousand and with our costs, that's barely breaking even.'

'Like all farming. One in three good years is awesome, but one in five or even seven isn't unheard of.'

Nick peered over at Jenny with an expression she struggled to read. 'What time are you due back in town?'

'Five.'

He studied the sun in the sky a moment. 'We better get moving then.' He pushed his horse into a canter. Jenny took a moment to do the same, wondering how he knew what time it was.

Chapter 28

Jenny sat below an air-conditioning duct alongside the counter in the airport, watching the arrivals display. Penny's plane was landed and would be at the tiny terminal unloading as soon as it taxied down the short runway.

Her mind drifted to her quick goodbye with Nick. A giggle escaped her lips, a woman at the counter gave her a strange look, as she recalled his answer when she asked if he could tell the time by the sun. It was the first real laugh she'd heard from him, making her stomach do flip flops even now. She couldn't imagine him looking more handsome than in that moment. Then he'd boldly admitted he'd snuck a peak at his watch first. It was something his dad used to do with the tourists, study the sun like he could tell the time by its position in the sky, then announce the exact time to the minute. Nick said it always made the tourists ooh and ah in awe.

The cool breeze of the air conditioner on her cheeks, brought back the scene in the escarpment. She acknowledged that Nick and Nev were right—the land ran with a heartbeat, a spiritual essence that seeped into her soul. The memory brought goose bumps to her skin, filling a void in her spirit.

No wonder Nick fought so hard to hang on to the property when his dad died. Was it another case she needed to consider investigating? She shook her head, telling herself that first she wanted to find out who killed Tiffany. She was surer than ever the girl met a nasty, violent end.

But even that could wait. Tonight she didn't want to think about murder, missing family members or possible fake suicides. Tonight she wanted to have fun and Penny knew better than most how to do just that and she'd missed her dry sense of humour.

'You look happy.' Penny walked over to Jenny who hadn't even seen her come into the terminal. 'Off with the fairies.'

'Sorry. I was....'

'Day dreaming. Who is he?' Penny teased, her wheelie bag rolling back and forth as she waited for Jenny to get up.

Jenny jiggled her keys. 'Let's go city girl.'

'Who were you dreaming about?'

'No one.'

'Bull crap.'

'I've just driven in from William Creek Station and I'm starving. I dined on museli bars and cold water and skipped breakfast and lunch entirely. I barely made it back after interviewing witnesses and driving two hours to meet you.'

'On your day off?'

'It was my cousin and aunt's case.'

'Did you find anything?'

'Don't want to talk about it now.' Jenny shook her head like a spoilt child and Penny grinned. 'Let's get you settled in a room and then we are off to the bar for some girl time.'

'Sounds like a plan. I've just got to load up my kit.'

****

It was just after six when the girls made their way into the front bar of the motel. 'I have got to find a place to live in town, that isn't the motel.'

'Why?'

'Because I'm sick of pub meals and I need some home cooking.'

'A shame you couldn't stay out at the station. They usually know how to cook up a storm.'

'Nick offered, but I needed to get back to you.'

'I thought you weren't interested in romance?'

'I'm not.' Penny gave her a knowing look as they approached the bar.

'Where's Cheryl?' she asked Stan who shrugged.

'Didn't rock up.' He wiped the counter down. 'What can I get you ladies?'

'So she was rostered on, but hasn't shown up?' Jenny pushed. Stan tapped his fingers on the counter as a burly miner in a trucker tank, with body odour strong enough to turn a skunk off, waited impatiently a few metres away. She knew Stan wasn't being rude, just busy and he wasn't to know she needed to speak to Cheryl about a possible homicide investigation.

'Sorry, I'll have a ginger beer.'

'Make that two. Alcoholic of course.' Penny added, watching Jenny closely. 'What's up?' She asked as the barman stepped away to another group of bar-taps to pour their drinks.

'Could be nothing, but I was going to follow up with Cheryl to see if she knew more than she was telling me. She was supposed to come to my room last night, but she didn't show. The other day in here, she looked uncomfortable when Len Holmes came in. I know she wanted to share more, but clammed up tight when she saw him.'

'Len, as in Senior Constable Len from the station here?'

'He's who I replaced, yeah, him.' Jenny shook her head. 'We weren't working tonight. That was the deal. Remember!'

'You started it.' Penny grinned as the two schooners of ginger beer arrived on the bar, dripping from Stan's slight over pour—that's what bar mats were for after all.

They paid the bill and searched for a spot to sit. The place was busy but Penny spotted a small table at the back of the bar, just alongside the wide opening to the restaurant. Nineteen-seventies vinyl concertina doors sat either side, so the areas could be split up if necessary, but today, the bar noise filtered to the restaurant and vice versa.

'So, tell me about Nick.'

'Not much to tell. He's good looking, rather unfriendly, but he seems to be loosening up a little bit.'

'How loose?' Penny teased.

'Behave yourself girl. I've only just met the guy.'

'Well, technically it's been a week. I've screwed in way less time than that.'

'Our first meeting wasn't exactly jovial, the second was hardly any better.'

'What made this one so good that you spent the afternoon riding out in the desert with the guy?'

'That was *his* idea.'

'So he *is* warming to you.'

'Oh, shut up and drink your ginger beer so we can have another.'

Chapter 29

Jenny held the door for Penny as they entered the station. Philips glanced up, a little surprised to see Penny, but grinned and waved.

'They sent the big guns from the big smoke again.'

'Just a routine follow up.' Penny assured him, then she wondered why they needed big guns. 'Is there a new case I don't know about?'

'Don't know. Just know Sarge has been tossing stuff around his office since I got here like he's pissed about something.

As if his ears were burning, Sergeant Mackenzie opened his office door. 'You two. In here!'

'Jenny.' Philips grabbed her arm gently to stop her moving away. 'Did you fill out a mugging report online or are you making a statement this morning?' Penny frowned, her gaze drifting from Jenny to Philips.

'What's going on?'

'Williams!' Sarge's foot tapped rapidly as he leant against the door frame to his office.

'I'll tell you later.' She turned to Philips to answer his question. 'No, but I will.' She rushed toward the back office.

'Close the door.' Sarge sat down heavily in his seat. 'You two are going to be the death of me.' His words were rough, but his demeanour said he was just tired. 'Why are you back here McGregor?'

No one ever used Penny's last name. Everyone just called her Penny. It was strange hearing it now. Maybe Sarge did it for added emphasis.

'Doc Holbrook sent you a report Sir.'

'I read it. You're on a fishing expedition. I get it. For whatever reason, you two think Tiffany Cox was murdered. I told you to keep digging and report to me Williams, not her.' He pointed at Penny. She went to protest she'd said nothing, but he kept pushing on. 'What have you found Williams?'

'I've only just got the volunteer lists from everyone Saturday Sir. I've not gone over them yet.'

'Alright, time to bring the rest of the team in on where you are at. I'll do the explaining about why I left you snooping around this.'

'Sir. I spoke to Cheryl Peterson again. She was going to elaborate on what she saw the night Tiffany disappeared and maybe tell me where she was living and with whom, but when Len Holmes entered, she went pale and stopped talking.'

'Len. You think Len has something to do with this?' He took a breath, puffed out his chest as he studied Jenny closely, trying to read her. 'No way.' He shook his head.

'I didn't say that Sarge, I just told you what I saw, but worse than that, Cheryl didn't turn up for her shift yesterday afternoon. No call, no explanation.'

'Shit.' Sergeant Mackenzie got up from his desk, stormed toward the door and opened it briskly. He stopped unexpectedly to compose himself, causing Jenny to nearly barge into him. She heard him take a deep breath before proceeding casually, yet purposefully into the main office.

Philips was sitting on the corner of O'Connell's desk, the Senior Constable seated behind his computer and to Jenny's surprise, Len was standing a few steps away.

He scanned the returning group with suspicion, then his gaze fell on Philips who didn't appear as happy to see his old work mate as he usually was. The puppy dog enthusiasm was gone and Jenny wondered over it.

'Len. Good to see you.' Sarge stepped forward, breaking the ice on the strange vibe in the room. 'Got a briefing to get through with the team, so if you don't mind, we need a bit of professional space.' The tone was casual and Len's expression changed to disinterest, but Jenny couldn't help but notice his eyes lingering on Penny. He knew who she was. She'd worked in town before.

Sarge waited for Len to leave and the doors to close fully before turning to face his team. All eyes watched him closely. Jenny knew what was happening, but O'Connell and Philips were puzzled.

Sergeant Mackenzie rubbed his hand over his mouth, squeezing his fingers together over his chin as he considered his words. 'I'm not calling it homicide yet, but we are treating Tiffany Cox's death as suspicious so get your thinking hats on boys.' He glanced at Penny and Jenny, suddenly realising the term wasn't entirely appropriate but no one was going to bother making a fuss.

'I asked Williams to run a few leads incognito, and before you protest, it was because I thought she was barking up the wrong tree and I didn't want to upset the locals.'

'He means I was the scapegoat.' Jenny added and Penny frowned her disapproval.

'Give us what you've got McGregor.'

Penny cleared her throat. 'The pathologist found Tiffany's death was most likely from asphyxiation. This was determined due to the broken hyoid bone in her neck and no other breaks or fractures consistent with a fall into a mine shaft. We believe she either died down there, or was placed there post-mortem.'

'Cheryl told me Tiffany was afraid of the mines, claustrophobic to be exact,' Jenny added and Penny nodded.

'Even more reason to believe her body was put down there to hide it. We also found fibres with the remains that have been tested and determined to be part of a South Australian ambulance uniform. There was a substance on the fibre which is consistent with cologne or perfume, and due to the higher concentration of essential oils, we are leaning toward women's perfume.'

'It could be Tiffany's perfume, rubbed off on the uniform?' O'Connell suggested and Penny nodded again.

'We considered that, but there was none of it on Tiffany's clothing.'

'We still don't know where Tiffany was living before she died. That was one thing Cheryl was going to share with me Saturday night, but she never showed for the meeting.'

'What meeting?' Philips' eyebrow twitched.

'I spoke to Cheryl at the motel bar Saturday night. I convinced her to tell me more about the night Tiffany disappeared and where she was living when she died, but Len,' Jenny peered over her shoulder to make sure no one was entering the station, 'Len came in and she shut up real fast. I told her how important it was we talk and she agreed to see me at the end of her shift, after eleven in my room.'

'And she never showed?' Philips squirmed. 'And someone tried to attack you near the laundry.'

'What!' Sergeant Mackenzie turned on Jenny, fatherly concern quickly replaced with an accusatory look that told her she should have already reported it.

'I was going to make a report this morning. I didn't know if it was related to Tiffany's case.'

'What else would it have been related to?' Philips studied her carefully. 'You said he told you to stop being nosey.'

Jenny knew now wasn't the time to explain her real motive for coming to Coober Pedy. 'I have been sniffing around a cold case. I thought it might be something to do with that.'

Sarge was about to ask more, but Philips cut him off, a sense of urgency in his voice stopping Mackenzie from talking over him.

'Look, I might be totally off beam but there was something about the guy who jumped you that made me think he was familiar.'

'You were there!' At least Sarge seemed calmer. 'Will one of you start at the beginning!'

'I was coming back from dropping Dianna and Tommy to the car. The kid was written off and she was taking him home to bed after our usual Saturday dinner and I was staying on for a few beers and the music.'

'Get to the point Philips.'

'Sorry Sir. On the way back, I saw a shadow moving near the courtyard, then it was two shadows, one was Williams—not that I knew at the time it was her tackling a guy who had jumped her from behind.'

'Philips called out and the assailant let me go. Ran like a rabbit to the back carpark, near the service entrance. It was pitch black except for the stars and moon out there—no street lights. We lost him.'

'And why did he look familiar?' Sarge turned back to Philips.

'Well, I didn't know why but,' he glanced at the front door again, 'I can't be sure, but after what Williams said about Cheryl's face when Len walked in and him coming to town when Tiffany's body was found...'

'You think it might have been Len?' O'Connell patted him on the shoulder. 'He's like a big brother to you. Are you sure?'

'No, I'm not bloody sure.' Philips was torn between loyalty to his former colleague and pursuing the truth. 'But the way he ran, the body shape.'

'Okay, let's get McGregor out to the mine for another going over. Maybe she can find something useful. O'Connell, you and I will bring Len in for questioning. We don't have much to go on, but let's just see how he reacts to a formal interview.'

'Sir. He's an acting police officer. He's going to call for a union rep and a lawyer the moment we bring him in. Shouldn't we find more evidence before tipping him off?' Jenny surveyed the three local cops as she attempted to make them see sense.

'Fair enough Williams. Philips, you and O'Connell see if you can find Cheryl Peterson. Let's find out what she isn't telling us.'

'I'll go over the lists of ambulance volunteers and see if anything jumps out. You good to drive yourself out to the mine?' Jenny asked Penny, who nodded she was. 'It's still a crime scene out there, so it's taped off.'

'I'll need a few of the S.E.S. guys there to get my gear up and down. I only searched and sifted the main area where the body was found last time. We thought we were dealing with an accident, possible date rape, but now it's murder, I'll need to sift through a ton of dirt for more evidence. The tunnels go back a fair way.'

'Do you want more hands down there with you?' O'Connell walked toward the door.

'No. I don't want anyone contaminating the scene. I'll need to control the chain of evidence from here. If I need more help, I'll call for one more of my team. Thanks for the offer though.'

'See you later Penny.' Jenny called as the group disappeared, and she was left in the office with Sergeant Mackenzie.

'You have good instincts Williams.' He returned to his office, a look of admiration mixed with anxiety crossed his face. The poor guy might have missed a cop who killed a local working right under his nose. The idea that maybe he'd done more than murder Tiffany must have crossed his mind.

Jenny pulled the files from her backpack, grumbling at herself for being side-tracked on her own family's case and Nick Johnston when she should have reported both her attack and Cheryl's disappearance earlier.

She sat down at O'Connell's desk, which she'd come to understand wasn't solely his desk, but a shared workspace they all used from time to time. The first file was the S.E.S. volunteer list, so she put that aside for later. Her main interest lay in who was volunteering as an ambulance officer for the Opal Festival.

As her fingers ran along the page, a cold shiver ran down her spine. It wasn't the name she'd been expecting, but it made so much more sense. With perfume and the pregnancy, it should have been obvious.

Chapter 30

Jenny fought to stop herself from rushing off with the information. Instead, she continued to scan the list for any other names that might be linked to Tiffany. Satisfied she'd found a new prime suspect, she did her due diligence and continued searching through the S.E.S. and C.F.S. volunteers list.

As she read through the names of S.E.S. volunteers, she stopped, the cogs of her mind rolling around like they'd fallen loose in an engine. 'No way.'

She snatched the two lists from the desk, rushed to Sarge's door which sat ajar and knocked rapidly. Every nerve in her body tingled as she waited for permission to enter.

'Come in.'

'Sarge. I think I've found something.' He nodded, she hurried to his desk, outlining the names she'd discovered. 'Sir, if Len is an S.E.S. volunteer and she's a prime suspect,' Jenny tapped the other name, 'we probably need to send backup out to Penny. The S.E.S. are assisting her.'

'I need to man the station, you go out. I'll call O'Connell and get him and Philips to meet you there.'

'On it boss.' She left the paperwork with Sergeant Mackenzie and sprinted to the gun safe. Removing her weapon, she checked it before snatching her utility vest from her locker and shoving the gun in the holster at her waist.

She was sweating by the time she reached the carpark, suddenly realising both patrol vehicles were out with the team.

'Shit.' She rushed back inside. 'Boss. I don't have a vehicle.' Keys flew through the air, she barely coordinated a catch.

'Slow down. Think! You're not a rookie Williams. O'Connell and Philips are on their way already. Penny will be fine,' he assured her. 'Now go.'

Jenny almost jumped out the door, running to Mackenzie's vehicle and pressing the unlock on the key fob as she approached. The Nissan four-wheel drive was a newer model than the one she'd borrowed from Marj, but everything was set out inside just the same.

She fired up the engine and tried not to spin the wheels as the vehicle surged rapidly toward the mine in a fashion that put O'Connell's earlier driving to shame. Penny was likely below ground and texting her while she was driving was only going to slow her down. 'Be okay Penny. Please be okay.' She spoke to the hot air around her.

Fifteen minutes later she arrived on scene to a sea of yellow and orange uniforms. At first she thought it was just the S.E.S. crew assisting Penny, but as she got out of the vehicle, the scene began to make more sense. Sirens sounded in the distance as bile rose in her throat and hot tears stung her eyes. She shook her head, resisting the urge to slap herself back to the emergency at hand.

She rushed to the edge of the mine, where a crowd of people milled. Others rushed back and forth calling instructions that Jenny barely heard.

'What's wrong!' She rushed forward, the entrance to the mine was damaged, the ladder to the shaft floor broken off a metre or so below ground level.

'We need to clear the area of all unnecessary personnel.' O'Connell yelled. 'Move back behind the crime scene tape if you are not senior S.E.S. rescue or police. Now!'

'But don't go anywhere. We need to talk to everyone.' Philips added as people began to clear some space. Returning his attention to Jenny, she noticed the crease of his brow and the thinness of his lips. 'There was an explosion.'

'No! Is Penny okay?' Philips was silent and Jenny's stomach knotted and rolled. Tears stung her eyes. 'I'll go down.' She began to take her utility vest off and move forward, her heart pounding in her ears.

'No Williams. You'll canvas these witnesses and find out who saw what.' O'Connell's voice was calm and powerful, helping Jenny focus and take a long, slow and measured breath to get herself under control.

'Was Len here at all?' she asked Philips quietly as she re-clipped her vest. Crossing to a group of witnesses, she continued to watch as two experienced rescue team members reset the tripod that dislodged during the explosion.

'We'll find out. Let's ask around.'

'Did Penny find anything before this happened?'

'If she did, it's buried down there with her. The S.E.S. team said she'd been down there about half an hour when the explosion went off.'

'Who knew she was coming back out here?'

'Maybe whoever set the explosion didn't know she was going to be in the mine. Maybe they were just getting rid of evidence. Mavis Carson's explosives were flogged the other day. He could have planned to use them for this.'

'He, being Len?'

'Not necessarily. Whoever took them I meant.'

'Let's ask if anyone saw Len this morning out here. We'll start with that.'

Philips nodded solemnly and went to the left of the group of onlookers, craning their necks to see what was going on inside the mine rescue area, now bunted off by the C.F.S team.

Jenny started on the right side, with a rounded, short man in his early sixties. 'Sir. Were you here all morning?'

'Nope, just mining up around the corner and heard all the commotion!'

'Did you hear the explosion?' Jenny took notes on her phone.

'Sure, but we get them all the time around here. It was all the loud shouting that got my attention.'

'Anyone strange hanging around the mines in this area this morning?'

'Not that I saw. A handful of those orange jumpsuits turned up. They started winching stuff down the hole and I went back to minding me own business.'

'Well how about you give me your name and claim number and then go back to just that.' The old guy grinned, a front tooth missing made him look even jollier.

She took down the man's details and glanced at the next witness, still scanning over her shoulder often to see if the S.E.S. crew had found Penny yet. She couldn't calm the knot that sat in her stomach like a rock, threatening to find a path into the light at any moment.

'Williams.' O'Connell waved her over as the paramedics arrived.

'Yes Sir?' She jogged over to peer down the mine opening that was obstructed by pieces of equipment that hadn't survived the explosion.

'This is Frank.'

'We met when Mr Pickard fell down here.'

'Busy week luv.'

'You could say that. What's up?' She directed the question to O'Connell.

'I need to stay here and oversee the rescue. You need to listen and then take Philips.' He nodded to the constable who was finishing up the witness interviews. 'Tell her what you just told me Frank.'

'O'Connell asked me who was on scene when I arrived.'

'You weren't already here when the mine exploded?' Jenny bit her lip.

'No luv. I'm advanced rescue. They only call me when the situation is serious. The team here this morning were regular volunteers, just handling the Forensic Department's equipment and assisting. Joe organised the team.'

'Where is Joe?'

'Down there I'm afraid.'

'He's trapped with Penny?'

'He is.' Frank seemed calm, but the corners of his eyes showed his concern.

'Let him carry on Williams.'

'Sorry Sir.'

'Anyway, when I got here there were supposed to be just two S.E.S. volunteers, but there was an extra.'

'Len Holmes,' she guessed and Frank nodded. 'We'll find him Sir.' She waited for O'Connell's approval. He nodded for her to go. 'You sure you don't need me here? I hate to leave Penny.'

'She's in good hands Williams and there is nothing you can do until we get this mangled metal out the way.'

'Philips.' Jenny called and the constable turned, saw her wave him over and finished up with his interview before joining her. 'Len was here with the S.E.S. team, without authorisation from Joe.'

'Damn.'

'O'Connell wants us to find him and bring him in for questioning.' Philips put his pad and pen in his pocket and pulled out his keys.

183

'Let's go then.' He started for the vehicle. Jenny went to follow, but stopped, her eyes glancing back as an angle grinder fired up and sparks began to fly.

'She'll be okay. These sandstone mines don't collapse easily.'

Jenny knew the sandstone that was indicative of Coober Pedy meant that no timber or metal beams were needed to shore up the ceiling. Digging a hole over two-and-a-half metres down meant you could start burrowing sideway and make a labyrinth of tunnels below ground without a chance of a cave in.

That meant that although the entrance to the mine was severely blocked by the metal ladder and the equipment mounted above the opening to lower Penny's gear down—the mine shouldn't have caved in. She only hoped Penny and Joe weren't in direct line of the blast.

Chapter 31

'Was Len still staying at the motel? We can try there first.' Jenny got the keys to Sarge's car out of her pocket.

'No, he'd moved out to our place.'

'Damn. I'll follow you there.' The idea of Len being back at Philips' home with Dianna and Tommy turned her stomach.

'Best you drop the boss's car back first. The road is crap. I'll meet you at the station.'

Jenny nodded and jumped in, starting the car, popping it into gear and dropping the clutch—a sense of urgency overwhelming her. The only thing she could think about was if Len was desperate enough to risk killing an S.E.S. volunteer and a forensic scientist with the police, he'd likely be high-tailing it out of town in a hurry.'

She pulled up outside the station and ran in before Philips arrived. A dust cloud said he was right behind her.

'Sarge!' She called out, heading into the back office without knocking. 'I've got,' she stopped, her hand mid-air ready to toss the keys back to her new boss and ask him to put a call in to the airport to stop Len fleeing.

'Stop right there!' Jenny's eyes darted around the room, trying desperately to take everything in. 'Unclip your holster.' Jenny's hand went to her weapon. 'Slowly!'

'You don't need to do this,' she coaxed.

'Shut up. Shut your smartarse little mouth up.'

'Easy Len,' Sarge offered calmly. 'How about we just take a second. What's this all about?' Jenny saw him flip the volunteer files closed.

'Pull your gun out by the butt with two fingers. Just two, and put it on the floor,' Len ignored Sarge, 'then kick it over to me.'

'What's the plan?' She did as she was asked, but tried to maintain eye contact.

'What's taking you so long?' Philips entered and came to an abrupt halt.

'Oh wonderful.' Len made a show of the gun he held to Sarge's head and Jenny was amazed to see how calm her boss appeared. 'You can take your gun out slowly too Philips and push it over here mate.'

'Don't mate me.' Philips' anger washed over Jenny like a rogue wave. 'You're a piece of shit.'

'Don't jump to conclusions.' Len's face contorted in response to the anger in Philips' eyes. 'Where's O'Connell?'

'Why? What do you plan to do?' Jenny asked again.

'He's trying to save Joe and Penny from suffocating you shithead!' Philips spat the words out.

'Don't be stupid. The mine has venting Danny. They'll be fine.' Len's hand twitched, but he didn't move the gun from Sarge's head.

'As long as neither of them were caught in the blast,' Jenny suggested and Len shrugged. 'Were you just hoping to destroy evidence?'

'Maybe.' Len's tone was calm, but his body was tense.

'So you *did* kill Tiffany!' Philips rushed forward. Jenny prevented him from getting past her, a hand firmly placed on his chest. Her eyes warned him to get his anger under control. 'You bastard.' His voice was menacingly quiet.

'You can't get away Len. O'Connell sent us to find you. He knows you were the one who set the explosion, so you must also be the one who stole the jelly from Mrs Carson.'

'She's quick,' he quipped—she sneered in return. 'I'm just going to grab those keys you so graciously offered and Mac and I are going to take a drive.'

'Where the hell to?' Philips pushed against Jenny's hand, which had found its way to his chest reflexively.

'Danny. It's okay.' Sarge remained calm.

'You didn't kill Tiffany though did you Len?' Jenny couldn't be sure but the volunteer lists placed him in an S.E.S. uniform the night Tiffany was last seen. 'But you did try to kill Joe and Penny. You did cover up evidence, stage Tiffany's murder scene to look like a sex crime and you certainly attacked me.' She was surprised at how steady her voice sounded.

Len hesitated, a look of uncertainty crossing his features. 'You think you're so smart. You're just a snotty nosed constable, barely out of training. What do you know?'

'I know we already have enough evidence to bring your wife in for questioning in the murder of Tiffany Cox. You can give us a statement if you like or you can run away, taking a police sergeant as a hostage. Then we'll have to send out a specialist unit to track you down, but we'll still arrest your wife and when the tactical team find you, they'll shoot a bullet hole right in the middle of your head for kidnapping a cop.' Her tone was intentionally condescending.

'You bitch!' Len's body stiffened, he was preparing to lunge, then his face calmed. *He was too controlled. She needed to find another button to push.*

'Do your kids have grandparents to look after them because even if you get away, you'll never be able to see them again and your wife will get, what?' She left a gap to let him think. 'Twenty, maybe twenty-five years for premeditated murder.'

'You're bluffing. You've got nothing on her.' Len was getting agitated.

'What are you doing?' Philips whispered over her shoulder but she ignored him.

'I'm not about to reveal everything we have, but we have enough to arrest her and I believe she'll be charged and found guilty. What perfume does she wear Len?' Jenny watched Sargent Mackenzie carefully. His eyes were calm and she spotted a slight nod, telling her to keep it going.

'Then there's Cheryl. What did you do with Cheryl Peterson Len?'

'I didn't do anything to her.' He was defensive now. If he didn't kill Tiffany, then maybe he wasn't involved in Cheryl's disappearance.

'But she knew about your affair didn't she? She knew you were the father of Tiffany's child.'

'She wasn't supposed to get pregnant. Stupid girl.' Len snarled, but there was something in his eyes. Sorrow maybe?

'She thought you were going to leave your wife and run away with her, didn't she? But then your wife found out about the affair, the baby. That was too much for her, the affair was one thing, but an illegitimate kid, that would have been humiliating for her. She held a tight rein on you Len, she wasn't going to let you acknowledge Tiffany's baby. So she killed her.'

'Shut up!' Len shook the gun in the air, removing it from Sarge's head. He raised it toward her. It was the break they'd been hoping for.

Sergeant Mackenzie grabbed the gun, flew from his chair and elbowed Len in the head all in one smooth move. Jenny surged forward, up and over the sergeant's desk, smashing into Len at full force and tackling him to the ground.

The gun was pulled free of his hand by the tight hold Sarge still maintained.

'Don't move a muscle you prick!' Philips almost screamed, his hands shaking with rage, his service firearm aimed at Len's chest, wobbling with the heaving of the constable's chest.

Len was on his knees, his right arm jacked up behind him. Jenny reached for his other arm.

'Hands behind your back. You know the drill.' Jenny pulled a set of cuffs from her utility vest and savoured the sound of them sliding and locking into place.

Philips stumbled forward, his hands still shaking. 'I trusted you. I admired you.' His lip lifted at the corner as though he were about to growl like a wild dog. 'Danny.' Sergeant Mackenzie put his hand on top of Danny's. 'He's under arrest. It's finished.'

Philips let Sarge put his hand on the gun, lowering the weapon and finally taking it as the adrenalin began to abate.

'That was bloody good work Williams.'

'Thanks Sir, but can we hand this case over to a detective now?'

Even Philips laughed a nervous, adrenalin fuelled chuckle, but at least he was smiling.

****

'Not exactly the Hilton.'

'Glad you can find the funny side.' Jenny sat down on the edge of Penny's bed and placed a card and chocolates in her friend's lap.

'She's doing fine.' Nev checked Penny's medical chart and turned to leave. 'You good for beers tonight?'

'Not tonight, I've got something on.'

'I thought you didn't date.' Nev laughed, but his eyes studied her thoughtfully.

'I don't.' Jenny grinned, Nev turned again to leave. 'Actually Nev. You said you could arrange for me to see your uncle and talk to him. Can we organise that soon?' Maybe it was time for Jenny to come clean with Sarge and Nev about her family history.

'For sure. Uncle will like you.'

'That's great. Thanks Nev.' The doctor left the room and Jenny turned her attention back to Penny.

'I can't believe you found that earring while you were stuck down there.'

'I thought I'd only broken my arm. But then I realised I sustained a concussion. I knew going to sleep wasn't a good idea so I kept sifting sand and searching the area. How the floodlights survived the explosion is beyond me.'

'Well, a fractured skull can make you do stupid stuff I guess, but that earring broke the case. Cynthia Holmes' house was searched and its matching partner was found in her jewellery box. That, together with the brand of perfume in her bathroom should seal the deal.'

'So Len covered up the murder and moved his family away?' Penny opened the box of chocolates and offered Jenny one.

'Yeah, Cynthia roofied Tiffany's drink to be able to lead her away and kill her without too much resistance. Len helped move the body, then staged it to look like a sexually motivated murder in case the body was ever found. In a way, I guess it was.

He's not saying too much, but surprisingly, he took responsibility in the end and if anyone was going to go to jail, it should be him. He hoped by doing a runner, and kidnapping Sarge, he'd distract us from discovering it was actually his wife who did the deed.'

'And they say chivalry is dead.' Penny coaxed Jenny to take a chocolate. 'What about this date?' Jenny smiled. She knew Penny would come back around to her personal life soon enough.

'It's not a date, but while you were unconscious a few days went by and I did a little digging into Nick's dad's death. I might need your help when you are back on your feet because I think Nick was right. There's something funky about the case and unfortunately Len Holmes was running the show at the time. Not that I'd expect him to give anything up, but bending the rules seems to be his gig.'

'Maybe it could help his case?'

'Maybe. If I can get it officially re-opened.'

'So you're on a fishing expedition into Nick's dad's death.'

'I want to help Nick and hopefully he can help me find out what happened to Melanie and Aunt Carolyn. But I like Nick, and breaking down his barriers while we work together could be fun.'

'You like him a lot then.' Penny shoved two chocolates in her mouth and giggled like a school girl, chocolate teeth grinning as Jenny gave her a hug, relieved her friend was alive and thankful she'd taken on the challenge of working in *The Opal Capital of the World*.

****

Thanks for reading! I hope you enjoyed *Her Buried Bones*. I'd love to see your review on your favourite online bookstore.

Her Broken Bones - Book 2 in the *Opal Field* series is available from all good bookstores. If you would like to learn more about my writing or what's next in Jenny's story, then visit my website www.atime2write.com.au.

Printed in Great Britain
by Amazon

22345648R00111